A *Pride and Prejudice* Novella Variation

Rose Fairbanks

Letters from the Heart

Rose Fairbanks

Published by Rose Fairbanks

©2014 Rose Fairbanks

Early drafts were written in 2013 and 2014 and posted serially beginning November 2013 and ending June 2014.

Several passages in this novel are paraphrased from the works of Jane Austen.

Dedication

To my Mr. Darcy who wrote me heart-felt
letters of the 21st century variety during our
courtship.

Mr. Darcy's letter she was in a fair way of soon knowing by heart.

-*Pride and Prejudice,* Jane Austen

Table of
Contents

Chapter One

December 10, 1811

Darcy House, London

8:30 am

F itzwilliam Darcy tore through the contents of his desk drawer again. *I must find it!* He lifted every single piece of correspondence from his letter tray. His usual fastidious standards did not help today, as there seemed no hope of finding the object of his search.

The letter was not on or in his desk, or among his personal files. He considered he may have burned it after all, but soon rejected the notion. His earlier drafts were crumpled and in the waste bin. Surely if he would have burned the final product, he would have burnt all the evidence. He could only face the truth and the likely consequences of his actions. The letter he had written to Miss Elizabeth Bennet the night before had vanished!

He called for his butler, who confirmed several letters were sent out last night in the last post. In an agitated manner he interrogated the housemaid who had tidied the room before he had arisen for the day. He decreed to his housekeeper that she alone was to clean the room henceforth, and only at his request. Additionally, all outgoing mail would be placed by him alone into the hands of the butler since obviously other members of his staff were too incompetent to carry out the task. If they had not served his family faithfully since before he was breeched, he would have reprimanded their mild look of censure; as it was, he knew he would be apologizing for his ungentlemanly display sooner rather than later.

Darcy dismissed them and slumped into his chair, pinching the bridge of his nose. *How could this have happened?* No, now was not the time to ask questions. He needed to make plans.

Yes, he needed a new plan. Darcy knew how to make arrangements and carry them through with authority. Groomed as a child to be the landlord and master of a vast estate, complete with wealth, smaller holdings, and many investments, forethought was fundamental to good order. However, he loathed admitting the truth to himself; his contrivances caused this very problem. As a Naval acquaintance had once told him, one could be too clever for one's own good.

Yes, Wentworth, I have been truly hoisted by my own petard: my very need to control and plan my future has, inexorably, resulted in the elimination of any freedom of choice: there was now only one honourable way forward.

There could be no more excuses or dissemblance, which he found strangely comforting; instead, he must plan to present matters in the most positive light. He thought back to how it had all came to pass the night before.

Monday, December 9, 1811

Darcy House, London

5 pm

"Are you certain you do not wish to attend the theatre this evening?" Charles Bingley queried his friend.

"No." Fitzwilliam Darcy said emphatically.

The two sat in the billiards room after the early and informal dinner. Darcy's younger sister, Georgiana, had excused herself early to write letters in her chambers, leaving the two gentlemen alone.

"I say!" Bingley proclaimed with a hint of his usual levity. "I truly had it right that evening at Netherfield when I claimed I never knew a more awful fellow than you on a Sunday night—and now a Monday—in his own home with nothing to do!"

Darcy remembered this remark and the surrounding conversation in great detail, but feigned ignorance. "I do not recall you saying such." He affected a scowl in hopes of the subject being dropped, but he could not intimidate his friend.

"Truly? It was after you and Miss Elizabeth were in a dispute over whether my impulsiveness was a fault or a virtue, and before you asked her to dance a reel and she refused you."

Darcy did not need the reminder; he had already spent hours with his memories of the twinkle in Elizabeth Bennet's eyes during their debate—*it was not a dispute!* He recalled precisely the expression on her face, the scent she wore and—to his extreme mortification—the exact shade of blue of her gown with the delicate yellow ribbon in her hair. *It was like the sun cresting over the rocky peaks of Derbyshire in a sky just after a rainstorm.* Darcy cringed again as he realized how ridiculous and poetic his thoughts regarding the lady had become. *I am practically a mooncalf!*

Despite himself, Darcy sighed at his memories. It was the second time Elizabeth had refused to dance with him, and he should have been offended, but she was simply too endearing. She had a unique mixture of sweetness and archness in her manner. Darcy had not met with her more than six times before being entirely bewitched. The time she spent at Netherfield, seeing her each day, had been a sweet torture.

His thoughts were interrupted by a sigh from his companion, no doubt remembering his own Bennet lady.

"Netherfield really was a very picturesque estate. And so close to London, Caroline could have no complaints."

Darcy closed his eyes in annoyance but knew the following conversation necessary, yet again. "Considering how frequently she claims to enjoy Pemberley and Derbyshire, it should be no surprise she cannot complain about the distance from Hertfordshire to London. I believe her complaints were of a different matter."

"Everyone in the area was very welcoming and kind. Caroline wishes to remain in London for Christmas but I had thought it would be quite nice to celebrate at my own estate, perhaps invite my closest family and friends." Bingley let out another sigh.

Darcy was growing alarmed. *He* had no desire to return to the area. "Are you certain you wish to host such a large party again so soon? You hosted a ball just over a week ago. You would not want to overexert yourself or Miss Bingley."

Bingley's brow furrowed and then his face lit up in amusement. "I am certain Caroline would perform any task to impress the Master of Pemberley."

Darcy groaned and walked to the sideboard to refresh his port. "Did you not already accept the invitation to Lady Tennyson's ball?"

"Yes. Caroline is desperate for me to meet Lady Tennyson's niece, Miss Howe, again."

"She is quite lovely and has a good portion."

"Her hair is too dark."

Darcy raised an eyebrow. "I believe you admired her hair and more in August."

"And her eyes are too small unlike..."

Bingley did not need to continue, and Darcy took a large sip. Blast the Bennet sisters and their eyes! The eldest had very large and perfectly blue eyes. Elizabeth had the most expressive and intelligent eyes Darcy had ever seen, a beautiful shade of brown that could turn nearly emerald green as well. Even the youngest daughters and the mother had a special twinkle in their eye. Yes! That was an important recollection—the younger sisters and the mother!

"Bingley, I know you are quite attracted to Miss Bennet, but you did promise to use this time in Town to consider other ladies and all the consequences." Darcy had privately vowed to do the same.

"Yes, I know. But what is consequence to affection?"

Darcy took another gulp of his drink and then decided to refill his glass and offer more to Bingley.

"The match would be lacking in all important ways."

"It is just like *you* to think money and connections are all that matter." Bingley appeared to be teasing, but Darcy still felt a bit offended.

"I do not mean only money and connections. You desire affection, perhaps even love, but you will not gain that with Miss Bennet."

Bingley looked sharply at Darcy. "What do you mean?"

"Her heart is not easily touched."

"She enjoyed my attentions!"

"She has a very easy way with everyone, quite a serene countenance. Do you truly believe she treated you differently than others?"

"I cannot believe her to wilfully deceive me."

"Did she declare sentiments?" Darcy was aghast at the idea. He had thought at least Miss Bennet and Elizabeth capable of proper behaviour.

"No, but surely she could see my intentions, and she made no move to discourage me."

"You are very amiable. She most likely thought you were engaging in an idle flirtation while visiting the area."

"You do not believe she has expectations of me?"

"Have any of the others?"

Bingley looked sheepishly at him. "I...no, their feelings were never attached, as you well know after this summer."

"And did Miss Bennet truly seem different than the other ladies?"

Bingley looked from the glass in his hands to Darcy's face and back to his glass. "I think you had better pour me another glass."

6 pm

"She never loved me. None of them have," Bingley bemoaned and sloshed the wine in his glass.

"You are quite young and so amiable you cannot see those who would scheme against you."

"I ought to be more like you. Or how you used to be."

"What do you mean?"

"Since we have returned from Hertfordshire you have danced nearly every dance at every soiree, accepted every dinner invitation, and talked with many ladies at each outing. Everyone is full of gossip that you mean to finally take a wife!"

Darcy grimaced. The last thing he needed now was London's gossips after him. His friend laughed at his scowl.

"Well, so it was until three nights ago. Then, you only danced half the evening and wanted to leave early, and have refused to go anywhere since. What has happened?"

Darcy sighed. "Nothing has happened. I have agreed to go to the next ball with you." He motioned toward the billiards table, "Please, let us enjoy our game. More port?"

7 pm

"I'm a catch aren't I, Darcy?" Bingley asked bleary-eyed.

"Of course," Darcy replied, quite a bit more in command of his faculties.

"Not like you, though."

"What?"

"Pemberley! You've got Pemberley!"

"Yes...too many want me for my estate."

"And your uncle, an earl!"

"You are a fine catch, Bingley."

He grunted. "And I'll prove it at Lady Tenley...Tenson..."

"Tennyson."

"Lady Tennyson's ball. I'll be irresistible."

"Certainly."

"And you too. Maybe Lady Elizabeth Harkin for you?"

Darcy scowled at the name. No Elizabeths. And she was blonde. "No."

"Your cousin Miss de Bourgh then?"

Darcy choked on his port. "Good G-d, no!"

"What do you want then? More money? Ties to the royal family?" Bingley laughed and then snorted, causing him to laugh all the more. "I know, love!"

Without thought, Darcy whispered quietly to himself, "No. I will never find love again." He peered at his glass with distrust. *Where had this sudden understanding come from?*

Bingley had not heard Darcy speak over his own laughter. "What did you say?"

"I will never marry for love."

"Right. Too silly for you. We must be dignified. We must not laugh." Bingley tried to affect Darcy's scowl. "No more love for me! No more angels!"

Sighing, Bingley laid his glass aside. "I'm off to bed while I can walk up the stairs."

"Are you certain? It is still very early."

"Yes, but I have had little rest in over a week."

Darcy only grunted as his friend exited. Willing the voice in his head taunting him with declarations of love for Elizabeth Bennet to silence, he drank another glass of port before an idea of sheer genius struck him. Ten nights with little sleep plagued his ability to think clearly. Then, in a flash of inspiration, THE plan came to him. Writing a letter of sorts to Elizabeth, confessing his affections would clear them from his mind. He would even keep the letter to remind himself of all the reasons he could never marry Elizabeth Bennet.

The following morning, as he finally comprehended where this ultimate, brilliant plan had led, Darcy ruminated on all the plans that had inexorably brought him to this impasse. Darcy had always firmly believed in planning, it was part of his very essence. He knew how to make arrangements and carry them through with authority.

He planned to merely advise his friend, Bingley, on his leased estate in Hertfordshire and recover from his troubles of the summer. He soon realized his budding attraction for an impertinent country miss and so he planned to keep his distance. But when he was thrust into her company against his will, he sought to find fault with her. And when he found her entirely charming and bewitching, he schemed to leave the country forthwith.

Upon noticing Bingley's attachment to the very lady's sister, and not perceiving the affection reciprocated, he planned to extricate his friend. He even realized the plot held the added benefit of never again needing to face Elizabeth's fine, captivating eyes. Bingley would give up the lease and never marry a Bennet. Darcy need never visit Hertfordshire again, need never come into Elizabeth's company on a visit to his friend's estate, nor see her in Town as Bingley's new sister. Yes, it was a succession of very well-considered, if increasingly desperate, stratagems.

Darcy shook his head again. He should have realized it could come to this when things went decidedly against his plans. He did not *plan* to admire the young lady whose beauty he had early withstood, whose manners were not fashionable, and who had connections in trade and the most vulgar family in the kingdom. He most certainly did not *plan* to fall in love with her. He should not have been surprised that, after leaving Hertfordshire, he could not cast out Elizabeth's teasing words and lovely face from his mind. He never *planned* to think of her day and night with increasing levels of distraction—even with a distance of twenty miles and the passage of ten days between them.

Before he met Elizabeth, Darcy could not remember the last time he was able to admire a lady as more than a dance or dinner partner. At this point, he could scarcely recall another lady's name. He should have known better than to assume his plans regarding Elizabeth Bennet could ever succeed; Elizabeth's appeal defied logic!

Yesterday due to the tension of feigning disinterest for several hours, and a bit more drink than usual combined with a severe lack of sleep, he was impressed with the prudence of his next scheme—writing Elizabeth a letter declaring both his love for her and all the reasons why it was impossible to ask for her hand would surely banish her from his thoughts.

Upon completion, instead of burning it, he planned to keep it to remind himself of his resolve. He immediately left the library and ignored the unease he felt over his decision. He would keep to his resolve. He had hoped writing the letter would give him instant peace, but he was confident reading the words again on the morrow would be beneficial. Although he retired to his chambers, sleep did not come easily. It was not until waking that morning that he realized he had a nagging fear that he sealed the unblemished final draft and addressed it out of habit. And now it was missing from his desk, clearly having been sent with last night's mail.

Now came the culmination of all his designs. There was nothing to be done for but write an express to Mr. Bennet, travel to Hertfordshire and initiate plans to marry Elizabeth Bennet. Her reputation would be damaged by his letter, and he was nothing if not honourable.

Darcy leant forward, rested his elbows on his knees and cradled his head in his palms. He took a deep breath in, then slowly exhaled and brought his head up. He could not help the broad smile from appearing on his face. He was to marry Elizabeth Bennet!

Monday, December 9, 1811

Longbourn, Hertfordshire

6 pm

Elizabeth returned to the house from an exhausting late afternoon walk after dinner. Several days ago Jane received Miss Bingley's note announcing the departure of the entire Netherfield party. Elizabeth argued at the time that Mr. Bingley could be no less sensible of his love for Jane or somehow in his sister's power to believe himself in love with Miss Darcy instead. Now, she began to wonder.

Elizabeth had based her remarks on the belief that Mr. Bingley was a man of independent means and thoughts, but now she recollected more about his character. He did have such an easiness of temper and want of resolution. Was he really so willing to sacrifice his own happiness? Had his regard for Jane died away? Or had he not noticed her attachment to him?

She sought out Jane and found her misty-eyed in their bedchamber, seeking refuge from their mother's constant prattle bemoaning Mr. Bingley's sudden departure and hoping for his eventual return.

Elizabeth began to abuse Mr. Bingley's inconstancy when Jane interrupted her. "I have nothing to reproach him with. He is the most amiable gentleman I have ever known but he will be forgot. My pain cannot last long."

"You are too good!" Elizabeth rejoined, but when Jane tried to compliment Elizabeth as well, the latter would not allow it. "There are few people whom I really love, and still fewer of whom I think well. The more I see of the world, the more am I dissatisfied with it; and every day confirms my belief of the inconsistency of all human characters, and of the little dependence that can be placed on the appearance of merit or sense."

"I cannot believe I have been intentionally injured. Mr. Bingley is such a lively young man; his manners give the impression of more favouritism than he holds. It was nothing but my own vanity which believed admiration to be more than it was."

"Most women believe admiration to mean more than it does, and men take care that they should."

"How can you expect a man to know a woman's hopes and fears? If men design to inspire such regard in a woman it cannot be justified, but unlike *you* I do not think so meanly of the world."

"I can agree to an extent. I cannot believe Mr. Bingley to have meant to raise your hopes, but there may still be misery without scheming. Some are thoughtless, some pay no attention to other people's feelings, and still others are too pliable."

"And which do you impute to Mr. Bingley?"

"Oh, definitely the last."

Fortunately, Jane did not inquire why Elizabeth felt the need to even mention the other two trespasses. Elizabeth left

Jane and allowed herself to think on the matter as was her wont.

8 pm

"But why has Mr. Bingley not returned?" Mrs. Bennet cried as the ladies sat in the drawing room.

Jane tensed and Elizabeth, sitting beside her, intervened. "The note from Miss Bingley suggested the business he left on might take quite some time to complete. It is not for us to know his life or to demand his time. We cannot expect so amiable a young man to find pleasure in our company alone."

Mrs. Bennet sighed. "He *is* so very amiable. Not like his disagreeable friend!"

"Wickham told the most dreadful tale about Mr. Darcy!" Lydia crowed and proceeded to tell of Mr. Darcy denying the handsome and amiable officer a valuable living.

Elizabeth understood that now that the Netherfield party had left the area, Wickham felt at ease to spread the tale of Mr. Darcy's true character, which slightly unsettled Elizabeth. However, recalling Wickham's words on the matter and his intelligence of Miss Darcy as a very proud sort of girl, Elizabeth found herself exceedingly vexed at Mr. Bingley. If he were so ungrateful as to throw off Jane's love for a disagreeable girl with money and great connection, then Elizabeth found herself believing he would deserve whatever misery befell him. Yet, she balked at the idea of him being truly so inconstant, and, considering that two sisters could have little sway over a man, Elizabeth determined most of the blame must lie with Mr. Darcy.

Her mother's wails continued on the subject, compounded with her anger at Elizabeth for rejecting Mr. Collins' proposal and the resulting calamity that would now befall them all when Mr. Bennet died and the new, and hateful, mistress, the current Charlotte Lucas, would cast them out.

11 pm

The rest of the house had gone to bed, but Elizabeth could not sleep. As was often the case, she wrote her disorderly thoughts down. Wishing she could converse with Mr. Darcy himself, she chose to write him a letter and imagine his response. Then her mind could rest. Surely puzzling out his character was the only reason why he was constantly in her mind.

Unexpectedly, her plan unravelled. While she intently examined each of their conversations and interactions, instead of understanding Mr. Darcy's character, she received a revelation on her own. She was hurt when he insulted her at the assembly because she was attracted to him as a handsome stranger.

At first Elizabeth believed him ridiculous, but too soon she recognized she gave weight to his words. To save herself from caring for his opinion, she found a reason to dislike him with every breath he took. Her reason could not tolerate her weakness in liking so ungentlemanly a man, which must explain why she lashed out at him as often as possible.

Despite herself, his intelligence and wry sense of humour appealed to her. The way he challenged her in debate but still respected her opinion made her feel valued. She had seen that he was proud and haughty, but something in her believed there was more to him, almost as though he wore a mask, as though her heart knew his. She could not fully explain how it happened, but while she was determined to dislike Mr. Darcy, she had somehow fallen in love with him instead.

I love him. The words were still barely a whisper in her heart; she did not have the confidence to allow them more voice than that. He looked at her only with contempt and had departed, taking his friend with him. Learning of his mistreatment of Mr. Wickham, his childhood friend, and his assumed role in separating Mr. Bingley from Jane hurt worse than his first slight ever could.

Her first thought was to burn the letter immediately. Then she determined she would keep it, for a little while at least.

Such a momentous understanding, that she dare not share with anyone else, she might wish to read again. Indeed, in the letter she expounded all the reasons she should not care for him. She could easily talk herself out of her fancy and firm her resolve when reminded of his faults.

With what she believed to be a renewed calmness of mind she readied her other letters to go in the morning's post: a letter to her Aunt Gardiner and letters to two local friends whose families were spending the winter in Town. She set her stack of four sealed letters aside on her desk and readied herself for bed, determined to sleep well despite her resolutely troubled mind.

Chapter Two

December 10, 1811

Longbourn

9am

Thomas Bennet heard his wife in the parlour shrieking with unprecedented enthusiasm. Although the man was rarely stirred to leave his sanctuary, he was able to discern the difference in her screams. This one had a tone of genuineness. He entered the parlour.

"Ten thousand pounds a year! 'Tis as good as a lord! Oh, I shall go distracted!"

"What are you speaking of, Mrs. Bennet?"

"Of Lizzy marrying! I knew she could not be so clever for nothing! And so sly!"

Letting out an exasperated sigh, as it seemed he was mistaken in believing his presence needed, Mr. Bennet rolled his eyes. "And to whom have you presumed to betroth her this time?"

"Mr. Bennet, I am sure I have no idea what you mean. It is not I who am presuming a thing! It is all here in this *letter*! Listen! 'Dearest, loveliest Elizabeth.' What else could it be but a proposal?"

Her husband snatched the letter she had been waving around and scanned the words with widened eyes. "Mrs. Bennet! How much have you read of this letter?"

"Why, I only read the first line before deciding I must know who sent it! I opened it because it's from London, and I do not know the handwriting. I hoped it might be Miss Bingley, but when I read the first line I determined I must know what gentleman the girl was corresponding with! This must be why she rejected Mr. Collins! So clever of Lizzy!"

"Who else knows of this letter?"

"It has only just arrived. I have not even seen Lizzy. She must be gallivanting off on a walk. I swear I do not know what such a great man can see in her. But perhaps he may introduce Lydia to a duke!"

"Mrs. Bennet," Mr. Bennet spoke sternly, but was unable to capture her attention. "*Fanny!* Hear me now, woman. You shall tell no one of this letter. I must speak with Elizabeth."

"Tell no-one? Mr. Bennet, we are saved! And it is such a fine match! I am perfectly resolved to forget how proud and hateful he is. I must go and tell my sister immediately!"

"You shall go to your rooms until I ask for you, or else you and the girls will lose all pin money for the next six months." By this time he was ushering her upstairs.

"Mr. Bennet! How dare you? This is no way to treat a wife! I must protest."

"Whether or not you must, you usually do. Fanny, I will not tell you again, nor shall I justify my actions. Remain in your rooms." He slammed the door before she could protest further. She let out a huff, but decided it would mean little if her information was delayed a few hours. Instead she drafted a letter to her sister Gardiner.

9:30 am

Elizabeth Bennet crept up the servant's stairs to her bedroom. The last thing she wanted at present was to be discovered by her mother. She had been unusually troubled this morning before her walk and took little heed of the mud puddles she walked through. *My petticoats are six inches deep in mud again, Mr. Darcy.*

Elizabeth shook her head; she must stop thinking of that arrogant, annoying, frustratingly beautiful man. She chose not to reprimand her thoughts for describing him as beautiful, for it was as true as any description of him. Opening her bedroom door, she had every intention to burn the letter she wrote the night before. Indeed, as she should have after she finished writing. *No, I never should have written it at all.*

Her eyes grew wide with foreboding when she saw her letter stack gone. The maid must have taken her mail to be sent. Attempting to stave off the alarm rising in her breast, she assured herself that no matter how agitated her mind was last night, she would not have left it on her desk. She must have absently tucked it in a drawer. She had not even sealed it and so there was no mistaking it for a letter to be sent, certainly.

For good measure, she recounted her motions before bed last night. She had sealed and addressed four letters. That fact was entirely perfect, as she had written four letters. *No, No, No!* She wrote four letters, but only three were meant for the post! Flying down the stairs, she asked the maid if the post had been sent.

"Aye, Miss Elizabeth, and the master has all the letters that came today in his study."

"Elizabeth!" Just then her father called from his study, before she had a chance to give in to the despair that must naturally follow the situation.

"Yes, Papa?" she asked from the doorway.

"Shut the door and be seated." Elizabeth looked at her father in confusion and consternation. His tone had a sharpness she seldom heard; it was as though she was being reprimanded for some grave error.

Mr. Bennet looked at his favourite daughter expectantly, but when she said nothing he decided to begin. "It has come to my attention that you have been involved in a secret correspondence with a gentleman of our acquaintance, though I am uncertain he deserves the title gentleman."

Elizabeth gasped and began to refute the claim, but he interrupted her. "No, Elizabeth, I have indisputable proof. Now, normally such things would point to a secret betrothal, which would be concerning enough, but in this letter—written in your young man's hand—he denies such a marriage will take place. I must say, for all that we have heard of him and observed, I never believed him so dishonourable as to correspond with a single lady with his name blatantly signed all over it. I suppose he does not have to worry about his reputation, and he must have no fear that I can demand satisfaction."

"I have not the slightest idea who you mean. I am not corresponding with any gentleman." The slight blush to Elizabeth's cheeks betrayed her as she recalled her mislaid letter.

"Do not lie to me." He pulled out the now-opened letter addressed to his daughter and waved it at her. "Here is the letter from your man, and your maid confirmed a letter to him was sent this morning."

Elizabeth's astonishment was beyond expression. She stared, coloured, doubted and was silent. Mr. Bennet considered this sufficient encouragement to continue, "Your mother knows of this and I am uncertain I can keep her silent. At least one maid in the house knows of your correspondence. Heaven only knows what the postman and his clerk have said. I cannot make sense of it. I thought you disliked him, which might explain *his* actions, but you wrote him. He vows he will not marry you, yet he publicly compromises you."

After a lengthy pause, he asked very quietly, "Have there been other compromises?"

Elizabeth cried, "Papa! How can you think it of me?"

"What am I meant to think, child?"

Elizabeth still could not credit what she understood from her father's words and chose to continue her denial, "You have no proof of my alleged letter aside from the maid's testimony, and I have not read the letter in your hands. I cannot fathom who you mean."

Her attempt at deceit could not prevail, for her father knew her too well. "I will not play your game, Elizabeth. Now tell me, do you truly hate him, for I think I must appeal to his honour."

Elizabeth gulped deeply and spoke to her folded hands. She could not meet her father's eye. "No, I do not hate him. I only wish I could."

"Very well, that gives me some peace."

"Papa...surely you have heard how he

has treated Mr. Wickham, and I know he has taken Mr. Bingley away from Jane. We cannot hope he will do the honourable thing. If this is known, what shall become of me, of my sisters? How cruel of him!"

"You mailed a letter as well!"

"But I did not mean to!"

"And why not?"

"I cannot respect him! I like him against my will and all reason!"

He laughed heartily and added, "It seems you both love each other against your will."

Elizabeth's head sharply lifted at such words, and her eyes flew to the letter Mr. Bennet still held. "Here child, I have kept you in suspense long enough."

Her hands greedily reached for the letter, and her eyes spoke her thanks. She ran upstairs to her room to read in solitude.

Monday, December 9, 1811

Darcy House, London

Dearest, loveliest Elizabeth,

Are you shocked at the forwardness
of my address? I should hope not, for
I dearly love calling you Elizabeth.
You will always be my Elizabeth.

In vain have I struggled. It will not
do. My feelings will not be repressed.
You must allow me to tell you how
ardently I admire and love you.

Have I shocked you again with my
declaration of love? I assure you it is
a true, constant love. I cannot fix on
the hour, or the spot, or the look, or
the words, which laid the foundation.
It is too long ago. I was in the middle
before I knew that I had begun.

How have you bewitched me? I have
seen the beauties of the first circle
and have remained unmoved until I
was captivated by your fine eyes
dancing not in candlelight, but in
mirth and obvious joy. I have
listened to the most exalted
performers in the land, yet it is your
performance that plays again in my
mind. I have conversed with women
educated by the finest masters at the
best schools, but not one of them has
your unique combination of

intelligence, honesty, wit and sweetness. I know many women whom are lauded for their kindness, but I know none who would walk three miles after a storm to nurse a sick sister, or forebear Miss Bingley's insults with such civility. I have been hunted in ballrooms since my youth, and you are the first woman of my acquaintance to refuse to stand up with me, and certainly the first to not seek my approbation.

This must be the answer. I love you because you are genuine and unaffected. You do not simper or seek to flatter. The ladies of my acquaintance may be draped in the rarest silk and costly gold trinkets, and tout many so-called accomplishments, but they can only repeat my own opinion. They are not authentic. You are the most delightful woman of my acquaintance, the only real woman of my acquaintance, as the others are mere figments of fashionable society.

But to one of these insipid ladies I will have to shackle myself one day to serve my duty to my family. Your connections in trade and the improper behaviour of your family could never find a place in London society. Though I care little for it, I must protect my family's position for the sake of my sister and my future children. And the ladies of the ton would be most unkind to you. I should hate to see you abused or regret a connection to me, though I rather think you would laugh at their folly instead.

In moments like these I must confess I would gladly cast aside my concerns about your family and connections, if only you showed me some encouragement. Instead you have fallen under Wickham's spell of charming manners. Tell me, what is it young ladies find irresistible about the reprobate? His ability to gamble away three thousand pounds given in lieu of a valuable living—at his request—in the course of two years? Or is it his attempts to seduce young heiresses into elopement, as he tried with my sister?

I should be angry with you. I should be angry that you are foolish enough to believe his lies, and foolish enough to doubt my honour. You destroyed the pleasure of our dance at Netherfield, which was supposed to offer me a lifetime of memories. Instead you brought up that cad. But I cannot be angry with you. He has deceived many, myself included. I love you entirely, even if you suffer from some misjudgements. I know you by heart – your errors are just further proof of your affectionate character.

I should be angry that you cannot leave my mind for a moment. You have invaded my senses, my every waking hour and each night as well. I want peace and respite from this, Elizabeth! Yet I cannot blame you. It is my weakness that leads me to love a lady unsuitable for my standing. You are not charming, intelligent, witty and beautiful by design. Your enticements are wholly natural and intrinsic.

I am alternately angry and relieved that Miss Bennet does not hold my friend in the same esteem he holds her. If they had married, would I meet with you frequently? Would it be enough to simply keep an acquaintance with you and to satisfy myself with a few lively conversations a year? Would I be forced to see you marry another and bear his children? Or would I claim the honour? And should I try, would you deny me even as you have denied me a dance?

I have made a mess of things, Elizabeth. I cannot see myself through this, though I pride myself in my superior judgment. Since I cannot see clearly, I have run like a coward, hoping the distance would remove the need to find answers, but it has not. You are here with me, Lizzy. You are in my heart.

Perhaps this letter may serve as a balm, and I can regain my composure. Perhaps after this confession I will be able to close my eyes and not see yours laughing at me. It may be that after I conclude this note I will stop searching for your face everywhere I go, remembering your words, and faintly smelling your fragrance.

It may be. I pray it is. And yet my heart tells me there will be none but you residing in it.

Forever yours,

Fitzwilliam Darcy

By the conclusion Elizabeth's handkerchief was sodden from her tears.

Tuesday, December 10, 1811

Darcy House, London

10:30 am

Hoping his friend was awake, Darcy sought and found Bingley sulking in the library. The evenings of the last ten days had not been kind to Bingley's constitution and last night, encouraged by Darcy's more liberal consumption than usual, Bingley had decidedly overindulged in spirits.

"I had thought to find you in the drawing room," Darcy ventured quietly, but still his friend winced at his voice.

Bingley shook his head and groaned at the motion, "No, I need quiet, and although your sister plays beautifully, it is not conducive to the ache in my head."

"I shall have Mrs. Redding fetch some powders..." Darcy began, but Bingley interrupted him.

"Thank you, no. I prefer the pain to anything else I might feel."

Darcy sat down and wondered how to begin what must be said to his friend. "Bingley, have you thought of returning to Netherfield?"

Bingley cast what looked like a sad puppy's attempt at a glower: "There is nothing for me in Hertfordshire."

Darcy cautiously said, "The estate is quite comfortable, and you should experience the winter there before deciding if you shall keep it."

"I am perfectly resolved to give it up entirely."

Darcy could see he must apply more pressure. "Is this because of your disappointed hopes with Miss Bennet?"

"You know it is! I cannot bear to see

her again knowing..." Bingley's voice trailed off.

"Ah, but we do not *know*. I only gave you my impressions and, even if I am correct, it is not hopeless. You could certainly court her and seek to gain her approbation."

"I thought you believed her mercenary!"

"No," Darcy stated firmly. He truly did not believe so. "Miss Bennet and Miss Elizabeth could never be mistaken for mercenary. I believe her heart is not easily touched, but yours seems still engaged. Perhaps you must try harder than you are accustomed to in order to gain her affection."

Bingley's brow furrowed in thought. "What of your and Caroline's other complaints? Her connections are not likely to improve my position in society."

"As sister to Mrs. Darcy, they will be quite sufficient," Darcy said, almost smugly.

"Sister to Mrs. Darcy? What are you saying, man?"

Darcy was resolutely silent, but Bingley's mind was suddenly up to the task, "It must be Miss Elizabeth you fancy! All that staring and disputing. I must tell you that is an odd way to court a woman! And it is *you* who shall have to try hard to win approbation, for she does not much like you!"

"Does not like me?" Darcy asked incredulously and felt insulted. *Perhaps she did not make overt displays of her regard, but Bingley sounds as though he believes she hates me.*

Instantly, Bingley was out the door of the library and racing up the stairs to the drawing room. Baffled, but amused, Darcy followed his friend. Georgiana was playing a lively tune, and Bingley grinned at the sound, his head miraculously recovered.

"I thought you felt unwell." In truth, Darcy was not surprised. Bingley was suddenly much improved at the thought of seeing his *angel* again. Darcy also felt an unprecedented lightness at the idea of returning to Hertfordshire.

Seeing his friend take up writing supplies, Darcy queried him, "Do you write your housekeeper at Netherfield?"

Bingley looked at Darcy in confusion. "Why should I? I am certain Mrs. Clark has our rooms prepared still. I had not yet written her that I was to remain in Town for the winter. We can eat at the Tavern if there is no meal to be had."

"To whom do you write then?"

"Caroline, of course. She will wish to see her friends again."

Darcy recoiled in horror. The last thing he desired was the presence of Miss Bingley as he courted Elizabeth. Characteristically, Bingley did not notice.

"She will not want to leave Town so soon, and she ought to stay here for the Season."

Bingley furrowed his brow in thought. "I should like to have a hostess." Bingley looked toward Georgiana.

"Absolutely not! She is too young. And she is not related to you— she could not be your hostess."

"She is practically another sister." Seeing Darcy's glare, he added, "We can sort it out later; it will take either lady too long to pack."

Rose Fairbanks

"When do we leave?"

"Immediately. Darcy, do you really think I can persuade her to love me?"

"Of course, my friend."

Bingley actually leapt from his chair and let out some kind of whooping sound. *At least one of us will feel comfortable with our in-laws,* Darcy thought.

Georgiana broke in then, "Mr. Bingley are you planning to propose to Miss Bennet?"

Bingley grinned, "Only as soon as humanly possible!"

"William, please, may I come?"

"Georgiana, I really am uncertain…" between exposing her to the Bennets and the chance of her meeting Wickham, Darcy refused to countenance the opportunity.

"I wish to meet Miss Elizabeth Bennet!"

"Eliza…Miss Elizabeth Bennet? How do you even know of her?"

"Your letters were full of her when you were in Hertfordshire. Or were you too

besotted to notice what you wrote?"
Georgiana laughed—actually laughed—at
her brother, causing Bingley to join in when
he noticed his friend's expression.

"I hardly think mentioning a new
acquaintance is..."

"William, really! Your interest was
obvious! My only concern is that, while you
were enchanted with your *debates* and her
lively mind, I worry she may actually
dislike you. I want her for my sister, but I
can see you will need my help."

Darcy had every intention of refuting
her claim and commanding her to stay, but
she met his gaze with what he knew to be
the Darcy spirit of determination, and he
conceded. She nearly skipped away to make
her plans, and Bingley left with an obvious
bounce in his step to order the carriage. As
his sister's words settled in his conscience,
it occurred to Darcy he was the only one
feeling any trepidation with the scheme. He
hoped it was only his continued
reservations about the marriage.

Fitzwilliam House, London

10:30 am

Lord Fitzwilliam stared at the letter he held in amazement. His nephew, Fitzwilliam Darcy, announced his betrothal to a lady of no consequence in the world. Immediately, he sought out his wife and found her sitting with his sister and niece, who had arrived in Town from Kent for the upcoming Holiday.

"Eleanor, I have just received the most astonishing letter from our nephew Darcy! He is betrothed to some lady from Hertfordshire!"

His wife exclaimed with delight and jumped up to read the letter as well.

Lord Fitzwilliam and his wife were too preoccupied with scanning the contents of the letter to see Lady Catherine's face contort in anger.

That lady knew she would gain no support from her brother and sister for her long-held plans, and so she quickly suppressed her feelings and coolly inquired, "Who is the fortunate lady?"

Fitzwilliam answered absently, "A Miss Elizabeth Bennet of Longbourn." He looked from his wife to his sister and asked, "Have you heard of her or the estate? What can he be thinking? I did not know he was even courting anyone!"

His wife answered, "Darcy was in Hertfordshire for several weeks. He has clearly fallen in love. You must forgive the boy for not informing you of his every thought." As usual, no one noticed when Lady Catherine's daughter, Anne, left the room.

His lordship resumed his puzzled observations, "It is so unlike him! He is always so fastidious and staid! He must not have known her very long, and she appears to be of no consequence in the world. Yet he has passed over all of the *ton's* fashionable and wealthy ladies."

Lady Fitzwilliam chuckled, "Of course, he passed over all those insipid ladies, he does not need them. And do you forget how difficult it is to command the heart? You proposed during our first dance, mere minutes after our first meeting!"

"Yes, but you refused me, dear."

"Naturally, I have always had the

most sense in this relationship." Lady Fitzwilliam's eyes twinkled with her teasing reply. "Now, write him our congratulations and tell him I insist on hosting a betrothal ball. I shall hear none of his excuses, and I cannot wait to introduce my new niece to our society."

His lordship left for his study to write his reply, and his wife shortly excused herself to speak with the housekeeper, already consumed with plans for the ball. Several hours went by before either questioned the whereabouts of Lady Catherine de Bourgh. Told by the housekeeper that their sister had a headache, they were not concerned until she did not appear for breakfast the next day.

Elizabeth reread Darcy's letter several times. She studied his every sentence, and her feelings towards its writer were at times widely different. At first, she was astonished to read that he was in love with her. That alone was gratifying and would answer the dearest wishes of her heart. But this sentiment was followed by anger as she read of his pride and false sense of familial duty.

In addition to insulting her family, he declared her unfit to assume the position of wife to a man of his station in life and called his love for her a weakness of character. Most alarming were his claims against Mr. Wickham's character and his confession of tearing Jane and Mr. Bingley apart.

But on a second perusal, she had to allow that her family's behaviour was improper. She weighed the matter of Mr. Wickham and concluded that Darcy would never lie about his sister; she was ashamed to realize how prejudiced she had been to have readily accepted Mr. Wickham's claims without proof. It followed then she was forced to recall that Charlotte believed Jane did not display her feelings enough. Mr. Bingley must have been persuaded that Jane did not love him, and although Darcy gave his opinion, it did not appear he did so with mean intentions. He even admitted that, although conflicted in his feelings, his friend marrying her sister would allow Darcy and Elizabeth to meet again.

The longer she considered it, the more she felt she could understand his reservations, even if she disagreed with his perceptions and mode of statement. She considered again the matter of his pride. Her eyes, now free from prejudice, saw more clearly that his actions and words against their union held some merit. While his manners were not amiable, she could truthfully only accuse him of being too quiet. Was his behaviour really so different from that of her esteemed father, who disliked society so much that he would rarely leave his book room?

Additionally, as little as he may care for the *ton*, he did owe it to his family—his young sister and future children—to not harm his position in society. He was willing to lay aside his ardent love for her, deny his personal satisfaction and desires, for the good of his family. This could be seen as an honourable sacrifice!

And yet, he said he would reconsider it all if he knew of her regard. She blushed at the thought of him reading her sentiments. Her blush was quickly replaced with agitation when she recalled her own written sentiments were not entirely pleasant. Indeed, they were more offensive than his words. How cruelly did she accuse him of mercilessly destroying her sister's happiness and of wrongdoing towards Mr. Wickham! He was worthy of every respect and esteem and yet she had rebuked him most vehemently. How heartily did she grieve every ungracious word, every saucy speech!

Darcy House, London

12:00 pm

Charles Bingley had spent the past several hours recalling his every interaction with Miss Jane Bennet and realized he was no closer to feeling assured of her heart. Of one thing he was sure after all the reflection: he was a coward.

His elder brother, Harry, was always self-assured and confident. *He* was Darcy's true friend. They met at Eton but became closer friends just after graduating from Cambridge when their father unexpectedly died, leaving the siblings orphans. Having recently been through such a hardship, including being given the guardianship of a much younger sister, Darcy paid a call on Harry, and their steady friendship was established. Two years later, Harry passed from a sudden fever, and Charles was left filling the void. Darcy readily helped his good friend's brother, and although the younger of the Bingley brothers would not see it, Darcy found himself in a deeper friendship with Charles than he had with Harry regardless of the difference in their ages.

Charles' father, Hal Bingley, had been amiable and good-natured and made all his new acquaintances forget that he was the son of a carriage maker. Harry was meant to be the first landowner of the family and was driven in his attempts to succeed at his task to raise the family's consequence. Charles was too easy going for such things, and many who knew him wondered if he might not just rent an estate forever and leave the purchasing to the next generation, but they were wrong. His hesitancy came from fear of making a mistake, of failing his family name, not because he was too happily settled anywhere.

And so it was with matters of the heart. The fear of putting himself out there and proposing to Jane and meeting a refusal or worse, experiencing an indifferent or unhappy marriage, paralyzed him. Darcy's words of encouragement allowed him to see matters differently. He would take on the yoke of his forefathers and be courageous and bold.

12:30 pm

Darcy House, London

The threesome was packed and ready for an extended stay in Hertfordshire when the butler met Darcy with the post as they gathered in the drawing room awaiting the carriage. Darcy still had not rescinded his order that all mail would pass directly from the butler's hands to his, either sent or received. His eyes widened as he saw the top envelope. It did not bear his full address—simply Mr. Fitzwilliam Darcy, London—but it was no surprise it found its way to his house. More shocking was the unknown and clearly feminine penmanship. Upon further examination the letter was postmarked from Meryton, Hertfordshire.

"Darcy! Did you hear me? They just announced the carriage is ready."

Darcy could not hear Bingley over the pounding of his heart. "Forgive me. I have urgent business to attend to." Darcy did not wait for a reply before departing rapidly for his private study.

He sat behind his desk staring at the letter addressed to him in a delicate, feminine hand. Darcy was terrified. He had not expected any sort of reply from Elizabeth. What was the meaning of the letter in his hands? She was not the sort to break with propriety, and there was no formal engagement between them...yet.

Darcy tried to recall the letter he had written her. Truthfully, he had written it for himself; she was never meant to read it. He could not remember the exact words, but suddenly understanding dawned on him. He chose to be harsh with the reality of the situation to firm his resolve to abandon the acquaintance, intending to read it at a later date. He made it very clear he would never offer for her, and she had no way of knowing he did not intentionally mail the letter.

Bingley's words reverberated in Darcy's mind. *She must be soundly rejecting my sentiments and improper behaviour. But why would she write and risk so much, only to berate me?* Such thoughts were unconscionable, and his pride demanded they turn in another direction.

Bingley is wrong, any lady would be flattered by my attentions, and Elizabeth is sensible. I have seen her embarrassed by her family. She will not be offended by my letter. Instead, she must be begging me to return. Fear not, my lovely Elizabeth; I shall declare myself properly quite shortly.

Encouraged by his latest thoughts, he boldly opened the letter.

December 9, 1811

Longbourn, Hertfordshire

Dear Mr. Darcy,

Twice now I have attempted to glean information from you to better understand your character and yet I am no closer to being reconciled with the differing accounts I hear of you.

I have heard from Mr. Bingley what a great friend you are. Yes, I see you are so very kind as to not have a care for his feelings of happiness, and to separate him from my sister, leaving her with disappointed hopes and in misery of the acutest kind. How can wealth and consequence replace affection and love in the ways of happiness? Can you be so lost to feeling as to suggest he marry where he does not love?

How can you be so unfeeling to your sister? What woman would want to marry a man while he loved another? Though perhaps that is more Miss Bingley's wish, to put forward one Darcy marriage that it might lead to another?

And now I do recall you mentioning Mr. Bingley's want of resolve. I do not mean to absolve him of blame, though you know his weakness and have showed no difficulty in manipulating his capriciousness.

I should not be surprised you can treat Mr. Bingley so meanly when I recall your mistreatment towards Mr. Wickham. You wilfully and wantonly threw off the companion of your youth, the favourite of your father, who had no other dependence but on your patronage and was brought up to expect it, for no other reason than jealousy of your father's attention.

But can you really be so dishonourable? Perhaps your actions towards Bingley are not proof of a selfish disdain for the feelings of others, but rather it does not occur to you their feelings may differ from yours. Perhaps Mr. Wickham has been misrepresented to you in some way. I am so weak as to try to find excuses for your behaviour. But these thoughts must simply be fanciful wishes on my part.

I find myself provoking arguments with you so I might find more faults, to remind myself of why I should not esteem you. Yet when we converse, I find you are exactly the man who, in disposition and talents, would most suit me. Your understanding and temper, though unlike my own, would have answered all my wishes. By my ease and liveliness your mind might be softened, your manners improved; and from your judgement, information, and knowledge of the world, I would receive benefit of greater importance.

To be truthful, I know no actual good of you, yet against my reason and my will I feel an unfathomable connection to you. I know you to be a proud and unpleasant sort of man. You have done nothing but give offence in Hertfordshire, giving every appearance of haughtiness towards our company and yet, this means nothing for I find that I love you.

And I hate you for it.

I could not be happy or respectable unless I can truly esteem my husband and look to him as a superior. How could I ever feel that way about you, with these faults in your character? You are the last man in the world I should be prevailed upon to marry, but I admit you are the first, and likely only, man I can be persuaded to love.

Oh! I am a silly creature. That I should even see fit to remind myself that love need not lead to matrimony when you have openly shown your disdain for me, my family, and the very community in which I reside. I even know you are destined for your cousin. However, all the logic and reason in the world cannot persuade my heart from breaking at the thought of yours never being mine.

Inexplicably yours,

Elizabeth Bennet

Darcy could not credit what he read. Elizabeth loved him! He perused the letter again, entirely uncertain why she had mailed it in the first place. Only to berate him? To declare her sentiments anyway, in some small glimmer of hope?

Darcy could not determine a satisfactory answer to his question. *It does not matter why it has been sent. My honour has been engaged, and I love her. The other letters have been sent, and the arrangements have been made. We shall marry. We shall!*

His reverie was interrupted by his butler's entrance with an express from Mr. Bennet. With great uncertainty, he read the message. It was as sufficiently brief, seemingly disinterested, and written with the same kind of wry sense of humour Darcy had come to expect of the man.

December 10, 1811

Longbourn, Hertfordshire

Dear Mr. Darcy,

I request an audience with you at
your earliest convenience. I invite
you to stay and dine with the family.
I do believe Mrs. Bennet has ordered
fish for tonight.

Yours etc.,

T. Bennet

Darcy wondered if Mr. Bennet would
have even bothered at all if not for his
favourite daughter's reputation being at
stake. The letter he had written George
Wickham, after the cur had attempted an
elopement with his sister, was decidedly more
forceful and less kind. Pondering Mr. Bennet
and all other matters would have to wait. His
carriage was ready, and so was he. He hoped.

Longbourn

1:00 pm

Thomas Bennet glanced at his watch and wondered if Darcy would have received his express by now. He was surprised when not many more minutes passed before an express rider was announced.

Tuesday, December 10, 1811

Darcy House, London

Dear Mr. Bennet,

I must speak with you immediately on an urgent matter. You may expect me this afternoon before dinner. I shall stay at Netherfield Park, so as not to inconvenience your family.

Yours etc.

F. Darcy

Mr. Bennet sighed with immense relief when he read Mr. Darcy's plans and realized it must have been sent before the young man had received Mr. Bennet's express. *Why would he come unbidden after writing he would not marry her? Mr. Darcy, you puzzle me exceedingly!*

Although offended at the man's words in Elizabeth's letter, he could easily see the sincere admiration Mr. Darcy held for Elizabeth shine through. Recalling his own courtship from many years before, he hoped the young man's affection was strong enough to ask for her hand in marriage should the letters remain unknown.

Fitzwilliam House

1:00 pm

"Good G-d! Can it be?" Richard Fitzwilliam exclaimed just inside his father's study, drawing the notice of his younger sisters who were walking by.

"Richard, we did not know you had come already!" the younger, Alice, spoke. The pair greeted him with a kiss.

"Yes, I am hiding from our aunt, what else?"

"What are you reading?" asked Emilia, the older sister, while glancing at the letter in her brother's hand.

"Darcy is to be married! He wrote father!"

"Married?" Emilia cried in disbelief.

"To whom?" Alice desired to know.

"A Miss Elizabeth Bennet of Longbourn. Do you know of her?"

The sisters shared a look and replied in the negative.

"He met her while visiting the estate his friend Bingley is renting in Hertfordshire."

"Hertfordshire? He has been there all this time? I thought he returned to Town recently." Alice asked.

"All this time? He is marrying a woman of six weeks acquaintance, for he has been in Town for nearly a fortnight now. Oh, how do we know she is not a fortune hunter?" Emilia interjected with alarm.

"Darcy would never succumb to a fortune hunter, but oh! How romantic to be swept away with love while on a holiday!"

"Calm yourself, Milly. Darcy has withstood London's most mercenary ladies and their mammas. Alice, you should know he could never be carried away by romance and infatuation. The attachment may seem sudden, but I trust his decision."

The scurrying footsteps of a frightened maid reminded them all of the visit of one who would *not* trust their cousin's decision nor find his choice romantic. Glancing at the clock in the study, they reached a decision unanimously.

"I will request our outerwear be brought to us and the carriage pulled around. Might we drop you off at your club before we call on our friends?" Emilia asked her brother.

Being the superb tactician that he was, and reaffirming that discretion was the better part of valour, Richard promptly replied, "I believe that quite the prudent plan, my dear, clever sister."

Alice snorted. "It is less a mark of cleverness than it is a matter of survival."

A short time later as they entered the carriage, they all smiled privately, for not only was their dear cousin to be married, but they had, not mere juicy gossip, but the finest hard intelligence of the year!

Darcy Carriage, London outskirts

1 pm

On the ride to Hertfordshire, Darcy's apprehension became apparent to his sister.

Georgiana placed her hand on his arm, pulling his gaze from the scenery out the window, and asked, "William, are you well?"

"Very."

"Truly? To me, I would call your expression anxious or nervous, but I have never known you to harbour such feelings."

"I only worry for you, dear. You are certain you will be content without Mrs. Annesley until she recovers?" Georgiana's companion had become ill overnight.

"Certainly." She grinned from ear to ear, a sight Darcy had not seen in many months. "I shall soon be in the company of five young ladies! Can you tell me about them?"

Bingley broke in with a grin, "Better to not ask him about some of the Bennets, Georgiana."

"Why ever not?"

"He does not approve of most of them, save Miss Bennet and *his* Miss Elizabeth."

Georgiana cast confused eyes upon her brother. "Is this true? Why would you disapprove?"

Before Darcy could reply, his friend answered for him. "He considers Mrs. Bennet and the younger daughters to be silly and vulgar, and believes that even Mr. Bennet can act imprudently."

Georgiana scoffed, "Methinks he doth protest too much! Can they be worse than our Aunt Catherine? How many times has she attempted to put you into a compromising position with Anne? And can Mr. Bennet hold his drink or does he turn into a nonsensical lout like the Earl? And let us not forget the Judge..."

"Enough, Georgiana." Darcy's tone effectively silenced his sister and Bingley.

Georgiana pulled out a book. Bingley began to feel the effects of his recent habits and fell asleep. Darcy turned his attention to his letter from Elizabeth.

Darcy finally allowed himself time to ponder Elizabeth's letter. He was quite certain it was sent without her reading his, and some of the smears indicated she did not write with ease of mind. There was a large blot next to her declaration of love, as though she wrote unawares and was startled by the revelation herself. It did not appear a final copy, neither were the directions clear. While this puzzled him greatly, he chose not to waste time on what he knew he could not answer.

Instead, he considered her feelings. She had every reason to dislike him. Whereas he recalled their debates—and he was firm in calling them so—at Netherfield as almost flirtatious, Elizabeth found only fault. The very conversations that showed her intellect and wit, which deepened his attachment, must have served to confirm her suspicions against his character.

He realized his manners, from the beginning, must have given her an impression of arrogance, conceit, and a selfish disdain for the feeling of others, and laid the groundwork for disapprobation. He could only pray that her dislike was not immovable and he could earn her esteem. He had very little hope. He doubted the love she felt for him, against her reason, was hearty enough to withstand the added insult his letter gave.

Darcy knew that he found it difficult to socialise in new company given his shyness, but he also knew it was often misinterpreted for arrogance, due to his prestige, and that he frequently gave offence. While he did not avoid conversing out of arrogance, he did not care if his reticence offended those around him. Elizabeth's accusations were formed on mistaken premises, but his behaviour warranted the reproof.

The fact was, he had disapproved of the behaviour of the Bennets, amongst other Hertfordshire society, and did not care to make himself agreeable. Georgiana's words were correct: his own family scarcely behaved better. He winced again as he thought of his letter. Darcy fervently prayed Elizabeth had never read it, and that Mr. Bennet alone knew of it. While it would do no good for him in the eyes of Mr. Bennet, at least Elizabeth would never have read his arrogant feelings on the idea of their match. *That I write of love in one sentence and call her unworthy in the next!*

After some time his thoughts turned on a different course. Elizabeth was not likely to be alone in her disapproval of his behaviour. Mr. Bennet was not known to be overly cautious with his family's reputation, nor diligent in his affairs. If Mr. Bennet managed to keep Darcy's letter a secret, there would be no imperative to marry to avoid scandal. Darcy had, several hours earlier, realized he would do all in his power to marry Elizabeth, scandal or not. But if Mr. Bennet disliked him, or even knew of Elizabeth's dislike, then he might very well refuse Darcy's suit, especially if he felt insulted by the contents of Darcy's letter, feelings that were only natural and just. The express he received from Mr. Bennet had been less than explicit.

The knotting sensation in his stomach grew when he recalled he had only managed to complicate matters when he planned to minimize any possibility of scandal by sending letters to his uncle and his solicitor announcing he had been engaged for weeks. *How presumptuous of me!*

His foreboding increased when he recalled he was missing a dinner at the Earl's house, and Lady Catherine was to be in attendance. Not only would she be incensed by his revelation, it meant Richard would be dining in the house; he was a snoop and a gossip outright. Additionally, the countess and his female cousins would gladly share his news widely! At the moment he was hard-pressed to understand why he had ever been so critical of Mrs. Bennet and the gossips of Meryton.

Neither Mr. Bennet nor Elizabeth was likely to be pleased with his actions. He knew not whether to race towards

Longbourn and demand his bride, or to slow in an effort to forestall the confrontation.

Chapter Four

Longbourn

1:00 pm

After some passage of time, Elizabeth determined she could not hide in her room all day. Hearing her on the stairs, Mr. Bennet called her into his study.

"Elizabeth, I have an express from Mr. Darcy, and it was certainly sent before he ever received mine."

She chewed her bottom lip to hide her anxiousness while her father continued. "He writes he will arrive this afternoon and must speak with me on a matter of great importance. I believe he will offer to marry you, after all."

"Let us not insist..." she desperately wished to marry him, but not if their marriage would harm him in some way; not if it was only out of duty. That was no basis for a marriage built on mutual respect.

"I must tell you if the letters are known to exist and it is presumed you are engaged, I *will* have to demand it of his honour, for your sisters' sake. You are being too missish now. You said you loved him."

"I do! But..."

"You read his letter, so you have seen our reports of his character were false. He is honourable. It will all be settled."

She was shooed from the room and did not doubt her father's words. She had come to believe highly in Darcy's honour. He would offer to marry her even if her own words killed his love, but the thought was bittersweet. If only she had seen his true worth earlier and had not been so blinded by prejudice and wounded vanity!

With such disheartened thoughts Elizabeth entered the drawing room, and soon thereafter Mr. Wickham and some other officers entered to call on the ladies. He began his familiar complaints about Darcy, but Elizabeth could not stand for it.

"I wonder, Mr. Wickham, that you were not able to find another parish."

He shifted his eyes uncomfortably and paused before answering. "My only contacts were through Darcy, and his malice was so strong he would not see me settled anywhere."

"Surely he cannot have such power over the entire kingdom, sir. Perhaps when my ordained cousin, Mr. Collins, returns in a few days he might have a recommendation for you."

Mr. Wickham winced, and Elizabeth continued. "I only thought, sir, it would be a shame for you to waste your education and what must assuredly be a vocation for you. If you have the opportunity to give sermons and get some part of your just due—after all a clergyman earns more than a militia officer—then it must be worth any pain to your pride."

He gave her a glare at the reminder of his income.

"For you would have spent three years studying for ordination and two years since awaiting orders somewhere, I believe."

Mr. Wickham's friend, Captain Denny, perked up then. "Ordination? I know I met you three years ago when you lived at Lincoln's Inn." Wickham stomped on his friend's foot. The following exclamation of pain brought the notice of the room.

He attempted to explain as all eyes focused on him, but sounded unconvincing. "Darcy had made it plain at his father's death, just as I was finishing at Cambridge, that he would deny me the living. I sought to study the law instead."

Elizabeth hid her smirk at how fast his story changed. "That would have been a very great thing for you, indeed! But whatever happened? How could you afford it in the first place?"

"I was given a bequest of one thousand pounds."

"I am glad to hear Mr. Darcy was not so hateful after all, to not give you anything from the will and that you were able to study. Such a sum must have covered all your costs." One thousand pounds to study the law was just sufficient but an *additional* three thousand pounds was more than enough for educational and reasonable societal pursuits alike.

"There is that...but the living ought to have been mine." He clearly chose not to address the fact that apparently he did not face the bar and could only blame it on his poor understanding or running low on funds and not finishing his education.

"I rather recall you mentioning it could be treated as conditional only, as Mr. Darcy claimed you rather extravagant."

She paused, and Mr. Wickham gaped, searching for something to say.

"But then, we cannot think so generously of Mr. Darcy. Instead, let us consider the good fortune his father bestowed upon you by ensuring with every lawful means you received the one thousand pounds, to give you such a start in life."

"Yes, I will forever be grateful for the kindness of the father."

"It does you credit that you have not forgot him."

Elizabeth gave Mr. Wickham a knowing look, and she could tell he understood her perfectly. Not many weeks ago he had vowed to never say a negative word of Darcy unless he could forget the good of his father.

Having heard the officers from his library, Mr. Bennet came and sat with them. Elizabeth cast worried looks to him, and soon he pointedly engaged in monopolizing Wickham's time exclusively for the remainder of the call. Lydia seemed displeased, but was easily consoled with attention from others.

When they had left, Elizabeth followed her father into the library.

"In light of Mr. Darcy's information on Mr. Wickham, what do you plan to do?" He did not look up from his book.

"Plan to do?"

"He is a rake and a gamester, surely a threat to our community."

At his silence, she persevered. "Please, Papa. I was so mistaken in Mr. Darcy's character and so willingly spoke against him even more so in the last week. Please, some redress is the least I can do."

Mr. Bennet sighed and finally focused on his daughter. "What would you have me do? Mr. Darcy did not authorize us, or I should say *you*, to say anything about Wickham –if he even meant to send that letter at all. He left the area without concern for us, surely he must consider Wickham no great threat to us."

"Perhaps...but he also had no connections in the area. It would be quite impertinent for him to tell the area's residents how to protect themselves from such an unworthy man. Nor could he say anything on Mr. Wickham's dalliances without risking too much about his sister. The whole area is very prejudiced towards him. It would be the death of half the good people of Meryton to find out that Wickham is a cad from Mr. Darcy's own mouth. Yet, *you* they may believe."

Her father groaned, and Elizabeth hastily spoke. "You need not be direct, after all you have no information of your own, but you are clever and well-respected. You can plant the seeds of doubt. How much is he spending, and how much does he earn? Is he known to treat the ladies respectably? Use his words against him. Why, only a moment ago I found many holes in his story about Mr. Darcy denying him the living with only a few simple questions!"

"Did you now?" he asked with pride.

Elizabeth smiled, "Indeed! I cannot think of how foolish I was to fall for it in the first place. If he were prepared for ordination then he would have done the necessary studies and been able to find work somewhere. If he did not study then what did he do between his godfather's death and the time when the living fell vacant, and how could he expect Mr. Darcy to give him the living unqualified?"

"Quite right."

"After a friend gave him away he declared that he realized upon graduation from university that Mr. Darcy never intended to give him the living, and so he chose to study law instead."

Mr. Bennet's eyebrows shot up in silent query, and his daughter continued. "Of course, how could a penniless steward's son afford that in the first place? He confessed to receiving a bequest of one thousand pounds, which ought to have been sufficient to study. I did not bait him further by asking him why he was not a lawyer, or telling him I knew of the additional three thousand pounds Mr. Darcy gave him, but I did subtly remind him of his declaration to me weeks ago, that he would not besmirch the Darcy name out of loving memory for his godfather.

"So you see, we just need to make some statements like so, and he will lose all credibility. Hopefully the merchants will not extend him so much credit that they are hurt when he leaves the area, and when others know he is not to be entirely honourable, they will hopefully defend their daughters."

"You might be correct." He paused for a minute. "And we have a special advocate amongst us."

Understanding him, Elizabeth suppressed a chuckle. "Do you think Mamma would like to visit my Aunt Phillips?"

Mr. Bennet laughed heartily.

"What is so amusing?"

"I certainly do know she desires to visit your aunt and tell her all about your supposed engagement as she saw your letter."

Elizabeth gasped.

"She only saw the opening declaration and then skipped to find the name of the author before shrieking in hysterics. She knows nothing of his other words." Elizabeth's cheeks burned scarlet. "I am uncertain we can hope she will not spread it abroad, but perhaps if we distract her with discounting Wickham in an effort to raise the community's opinion of Mr. Darcy that will work for the afternoon. After all, he may be as 'good as a Lord' as she put it, but she would certainly want you to be the envy of the county and not just for his riches."

"Papa, he may not offer for me and there may be no need otherwise..."

"Fine, fine. Have it your way, but I find it excessively amusing that we may rid the county of Wickham and save your Mr. Darcy's reputation through the silliness of your mother."

He meant it as a jest, but Elizabeth could not help but recall Darcy's rather just accusations of the impropriety of her family and blushed again. "As useful as that trait will be in this case, you must see it is not always so. My mother means well but can do material harm to our credit, especially as my youngest sisters are allowed to go unchecked. I cannot but think that if he had not so despised our family's behaviour he might not have counselled Mr. Bingley on leaving the area. Even if they both believed Jane indifferent, her affections might have been won or even deemed bearable if not accompanied by such vulgar relations. No, it was not her modesty which is to blame, but the actions of her own family, myself included."

"Such squeamish youths."

"Squeamish! Men of sense do not want to be connected to a family prone to disaster. Were we not just speaking of the misfortunes that could befall a lady who accepts Mr. Wickham's attentions? Do you really believe your daughters somehow immune from such charms? And not just him, but any man willing enough to give them the attention and affection they find lacking elsewhere?"

Suddenly realizing what she implied, she quit speaking. She expected to see her father angry, but instead saw sad acknowledgement, resignation and guilt on his face.

"Forgive me."

"No, no. I have at last seen that I must be cautious. I will speak with your mother, and we will begin a course of improvement."

Humbled that he could take her opinion so readily, Elizabeth gazed at her hands. "Thank you."

"Now, I am certain you will wish to accompany your mother, so round up your sisters while I go and explain to her why we must save your young man's reputation."

"Papa, please. No more teasing. You read his letter. His senses were addled. If we can prevent the gossip, then there is no reason for him to marry me. I do this only because it is required of my honour."

She left the room and did not hear her father mumble, "I recall perfectly well being in love against my will five and twenty years ago, my dear. Make no mistake about it, he does love you and will come and take you away from me."

Shaking his head from his reverie, Mr. Bennet ascended the stairs to his wife's chambers. He had barely entered them in the last ten years at least, but it was time to face what he could not change. He knocked on the door and was surprised when she opened it directly.

"Mr. Bennet!" she peered down the hallway as though she expected someone else.

"Fanny, may I come in? We must discuss very serious matters."

Her eyes widened at his words, and she allowed him to enter. He led her to the sofa in her dressing room before beginning.

"Fanny, I apologize for sending you away earlier when you found Lizzy's letter."

"As well you should! This is just the time she needs her mother, to set everything up for her. She can have no use for you at all until Mr. Darcy comes to get your blessing."

For the first time in years, Mr. Bennet paid attention to his wife's words.

He would address that matter later, but for now he must speak with her on his daughter's erstwhile lover.

"Fanny, it is Mr. Darcy coming to ask for my blessing I must speak on." He paused, feeling the guilt of his trespasses against his family. "You did not read more of the letter, did you?"

Mrs. Bennet shook her head, and he continued. "Mr. Darcy was not proposing."

"Not proposing!" she shrieked. "Not proposing! Why, he has written Lizzy a love letter! The postman will have seen it, and you know Mrs. Long hovers nearby all day to hear gossip. And the servants! What does he want with her then? Oh, we are ruined! That headstrong, foolish girl! Nobody will believe that we were used so ill by him. He must think he can do whatever he pleases, he is so high and mighty!"

Taking her hand in his, Mr. Bennet spoke calmly. "Mr. Darcy has since written that he will arrive, and I will ask why he sent the first letter. I do believe it was quite some mistake though. You see, gentlemen may be in love and it not always lead to matrimony."

Her shrieks turned to wails. "Yes, as we know with Mr. Bingley!"

"My dear, listen to me. A prudent man, one who would be worthy of our daughters and to whom I would give my consent, must think seriously about things. Our daughters have little money."

"That entail! The dreadful Collins and now Charlotte Lucas to come and usurp our place!"

Ignoring her outburst, he continued. "And we have neglected their education. They have little but their charms to recommend them."

"Neglected their education? Why, they are some of the most accomplished young ladies in our community! And all so fair! Charms indeed!"

"This pales in comparison to what men of Society may often find elsewhere."

"Jane paling in comparison to someone! Impossible."

"These new gentlemen we have met also associate with families of rank and circumstance."

"Ah! So Mr. Darcy is too full of pride. He claims to love our Lizzy, but not enough to overlook an uncle in trade. And he took Mr. Bingley with him?"

"It is more than that. He worries about the behaviour of our family."

Mr. Bennet knew this would be the most painful news of all to tell his wife. She prided herself on becoming a gentleman's wife and on being a good mistress of one of the larger estates in the area. She was excessively defensive about her family's origins, but to be told that they lacked in decorum was almost too much, he was certain. She was entirely speechless, her lip quivering and her face showing confusion.

"We have indulged our younger daughters too much as we were distracted by our own troubles. We ought to have hired a governess or been stricter with them. We have allowed them to be overrun with sensibility."

"What do you mean to say, Mr. Bennet?"

"Mr. Darcy is coming to meet with me. I do not know if he will offer for Lizzy, whether or not the letters are known. I do not know if she will accept him if they are unknown."

"She would not dream of refusing *him!*"

"I am rather sure she would."

"Does she hate him so much? He loves her! How can she refuse a man who can offer her so much?"

"Lizzy has never cared for wealth and splendour."

"But she does want esteem and love! I could not... Well, what is it you are asking of me?"

"I might persuade Mr. Darcy to stay in the area, until we are certain no gossip arises. During that time, perhaps we can improve his impression of our family, which I believe both Lizzy and Mr. Darcy consider an obstacle. Lydia and Kitty are not to be so flirtatious. Mr. Darcy's letter also contained information about a new acquaintance of ours. It transpires that Wickham is a wild young man, a gamester and a seducer. He will not be welcome in my home again, and if I hear of my daughters speaking with him above the barest of civilities they will be harshly punished."

Mrs. Bennet gasped. "He is such a charming young man! No, it must be some dreadful misunderstanding between him and Mr. Darcy."

"You must pick your champion, madam. Either you desire Mr. Darcy to marry Lizzy or you will stand beside Wickham. He has abused the Darcys terribly and I fear if we stand beside him Mr. Darcy will never align himself with our family. You were in the room during Wickham's call. He could barely keep his lies together."

"There is that..."

"It is not just Wickham. Any of the officers may be wearing a facade of gentlemanly character. I will not entirely revoke Kitty and Lydia's ability to enjoy amusements with their sisters, but there is to be no hopes of serious courtships and marriage for them."

"But, the entail! How can you not think of us!"

"If Mr. Darcy marries Lizzy, I daresay you will be set up nicely after I am gone. Even more so if Mr. Bingley returns with him and offers for Jane. I would rather my daughters have to be taken-in by family than be pushed into unhappy alliances, and if any are seduced by scoundrels because they are out too young without the proper attention of their parents, then we are all ruined."

The marriage of her five daughters had been Mrs. Bennet's dearest wish since Jane was fifteen. She was now thrown into a state of shock and hardly knew what to do with herself, with two on the verge of matrimony and another two she could not fuss over.

"Now, you said earlier that an engagement is a time when a daughter needs her mother."

"Yes, but I have nothing to plan, do I?"

"No, but we can improve our younger daughters and, if not these men, in time other suitors will arise. More than that, there is a task for you today."

"Lizzy has convinced me that it is unfair for Mr. Darcy to return to the area with everyone hating him due to our own prejudice and Wickham's lies, and for the town to be a victim to Wickham's ways. She hopes you and your sister Phillips will be beneficial in turning our Society's opinion of both men. Indeed, between you and I, such a change may improve Mr. Darcy's opinion of us as well!"

A twinkle emerged in Mrs. Bennet's eyes. "Oh! I would like that. Well, certainly it shall only be the work of a moment! Hill!"

Mr. Bennet laughed at her enthusiasm. "One more thing, my dear. Have you felt...lonely? Useless? Since our girls have grown up? Is that one of the reasons you have been so excited by the prospect of their marriages? A girl does need her mother at such times."

A tear slid down Mrs. Bennet's cheek. "Oh! You have been locked away in your library and refused to see how they have grown up. And ... and since I was unable to give you more children and an heir, I have been so melancholy seeing them grow. So nervous over our futures. And I thought I was doing the right thing hoping they would marry well. Is that not what a good mother does?"

He drew her close, wiped her tear, and then kissed her forehead. "You are a very affectionate mother. I have wronged you by staying away from you, from the girls, but I could not bear my weakness."

"Your weakness? All these years I thought you were disappointed in me! That I could not give you a son nor was I clever enough for you."

"No, dearest. You might not be very clever, but you were my happy wife for many years. I saw how your anxieties grew but knew no way to ease them. Instead of talking with you plainly, I chose to hide until the storm passed, but it never did."

"I have been very silly; caring more for gossip and the opinions of women in an effort to ignore the opinion of my own husband. You must regret your moment of infatuation which led to our marriage."

She hung her head low, and Mr. Bennet raised her chin. "I can never regret our marriage—look at our girls! I regret some of my actions, or inaction, during our marriage. I regret that I did not listen to you better, that I did not respect you enough to understand your concerns and cares. I still know you by heart. Let us show our girls a better way now."

"Truly, Thomas?"

He smiled at the name she had not called him in years. "Yes, Fanny. Now, get dressed for you are to call on your sister with the girls, and we can begin to mend our errors."

Chapter Five

Longbourn

1:30 pm

Jane Bennet saw her father and dearest sister leave the library. Curiously, her father went upstairs, and she heard him stop at the door she knew to be her mother's. Before she could ponder what that could be about, Elizabeth approached her, clearly discomfited.

"Lizzy, are you well?" She looked as

though she had not slept much lately. Few would guess from Jane's countenance but the same was true for her.

"I hope to be, I hope to be," was the only muttered reply she received.

Jane allowed Elizabeth a moment, knowing that in time whatever discouraged her sister she would overcome, if given a moment's reflection.

Elizabeth's confusion and unease cleared, and she drew herself up. "Jane, help me gather our sisters. We are to go to town to visit our aunt. We have important news to share."

"News?" How unlike Elizabeth to wish to gossip!

"We were fooled by Mr. Wickham, I more than anyone else. He is a liar and a rake. Papa and I have determined to tell the area the truth of him and defend poor Mr. Darcy's name."

"Poor Mr. Darcy? Mr. Wickham so awful?" She put her hand to Elizabeth's forehead. Surely she must be ill.

Elizabeth swatted Jane's hand away. "Help me, please."

"I can hardly help if I do not understand. What has happened? How can you know this of Mr. Wickham and why are you now protecting Mr. Darcy?"

Elizabeth let out a frustrated sigh. "Mr. Darcy wrote a letter...detailing the truth of Wickham. Such things as Wickham has done, Mr. Darcy would have no reason to lie about."

"That is why you were speaking to him so! I was surprised we had not noticed the error in his story before, but then he must not want to admit how difficult he found studying the law to be."

"He spent the money he received from his godfather *and* was compensated three thousand pounds for giving up the promised living *by his own request*. Even if he were a poor student and felt he must make his income elsewhere, he should have had plenty left over to buy a very nice commission. Instead, he must have gambled it all away!"

Jane gasped. Had they truly been so deceived? "My dear sister, can you be certain? Only yesterday you were certain Mr. Darcy used Wickham so badly. There must be some dreadful misunderstanding between them."

"Do you not see there is only enough evidence to make one good sort of man. You may think as you please, but I am certain it is all on Darcy's side and mean to let the neighbourhood know my mistake."

Jane thought seriously for a moment. Her sister had always been stubborn and inflexible and yet she had very quickly changed her opinion on this matter. It seemed as though her father agreed. Surely he understood the particular of Mr. Darcy's letter better than even Elizabeth did. It pained her to think so amiable a young man could be so terrible, yet she had recently learned another amiable young man could think so little of her feelings. She would not say she was treated cruelly by him or injured intentionally, but his sudden abandonment had hurt her immensely; she would learn from her mistake. A handsome face and charming manners could not be entirely trusted. If her father and sister, who both had exceptional sense, were certain of this path, then she would support them.

"Very well, but what are we to explain to our sisters? They are enamoured of Mr. Wickham! Nearly every girl in the area is out of her senses over him!"

"But why are they so enamoured? Because they think he's handsome and charming? Well, his looks we can do nothing about, but even the silliest lady does not want a dissolute husband. Even Lydia would pay some attention to money and not only is he poor to start with, but he spends far more than he has."

"But can you expect a girl in love to have so much more sense than her peers?"

She began to cry as a sudden revelation struck her. Bingley may have all kinds of sensible reasons to not marry her, but if he were truly in love would they matter at all? And what of her? If he returned today would she still love him despite losing her respect for him? It would hardly be sensible to trust him or marry him after such capriciousness, but then why wonder this at all? Bingley was not to return this day, and her decision may never be required as a thousand things may arise between now and the summer to drive her from his mind. But oh! How she hated to feel a fool and as though her vanity had led her astray. She could only hope time would also drive him from her mind.

Elizabeth embraced and calmed her. After drying Jane's eyes, Elizabeth spoke.

"There my dear sister. We shall be well. As you say, the pain will not last. They shall be forgot."

Before being able to ask her sister just what she meant, she was tugged into the drawing room to help gather her sisters.

"We are to go and visit our Aunt Phillips when our mother comes down. Come, let us ready ourselves."

"It is not our day to visit our Aunt! We always stay home on Tuesdays to receive callers! More officers may come!" Lydia complained.

"Yes! We have not seen Carter or Saunderson, yet," Kitty agreed.

"Do you not wonder why some of the officers are so idle that they can spare time to visit us so frequently?" Elizabeth cried in vexation.

"Idle! Plenty of men and women do nothing but visit and gossip." Kitty returned.

"But they are gentlemen and ladies of *leisure* whilst an officer must earn his income, and he can scarcely hope to distinguish himself if he is never at task."

"Colonel Forster visits and entertains very frequently! He is even to be married!" Lydia exclaimed.

"And how old is the colonel, Lyddie? How long, even in a time of war, has it taken for him to save enough money to purchase a colonel's position? Or if he has had it for many years, why not purchase a greater one? Do you not notice all the other officers are unmarried? They cannot afford it, and you better not be taken in by someone only promising love but never any bread on the table let alone ribbons for your hair and shoe roses for dancing. More likely you would be mending their uniforms and washing their smalls!"

"La! Who notices those things when you are in love? Lizzy, you begin to sound like Charlotte Lucas wanting to count a man's purse before accepting his suit!"

Before she could reply, Mary broke in. "Love and infatuation are very different things. All that I have read convinces me that it is so. Infatuation lacks all sound judgement and is often times so extravagant it cannot last. Love requires great constancy for we are told husbands must love their wives as Christ did the church, as He laid down His life for it. An unselfish loyalty is the motivation of love."

Kitty rolled her eyes. "Nobody wants your sermons on love! Lizzy, tell us more about your secret beau then. Someone must have caught your eye if you suddenly dislike the company of the officers. I know! It must be Mr. Darcy! Well, he's got money enough for you then, and the rest of us can be as foolish as we like."

Elizabeth's cheeks burned scarlet, and Jane was surprised to hear such a poor attempt at logic from her Kitty and Lydia. Had they always been so ridiculous?

"Oh, yes! That will do very well. Mr. Darcy can read to you in Greek every night before you are to go to bed!" Lydia and Kitty giggled, and Mary glared harshly at them.

"Enough!" Jane cried forcefully, startling the entire room. "You have had nothing but love, flirtation and officers in your head for far too long now. Ask yourself how you could even be a wife. Do you not see Mamma going over the accounts and planning meals with Cook? You must learn to think on serious subjects or I should suggest you go back to the schoolroom! You, too, Kitty."

Kitty fairly whimpered, and even Lydia was astonished at their eldest sister's tone. Jane trembled at her discomposure.

She had never let herself feel anything so intense before in her life.

"Bravo! That is the most unforgiving speech you have ever made." Elizabeth's praise made the tension break, and all the sisters lightly laughed.

At that moment they heard their parents on the stairs.

"I do believe, Mrs. Bennet, that we have some of the silliest daughters in the country."

"Mr. Bennet! How you tease!"

Such words were often said at Longbourn, but this time the tones of the speakers were so different that they drew the notice of all five daughters. Mr. Bennet took advantage of their attention.

"Girls, sit and listen," he spoke with unprecedented authority.

To Jane's amazement all her sisters obeyed.

"I must explain some news regarding an acquaintance. Mr. Wickham is not to be trusted and not to enter our home again. He has entertained us with lies and means to swindle the good people of our town from their money and their *virtue*." He paused and looked each daughter in her eyes as they all blushed.

"Today we shall go to town and make his character known. I have had word, and Elizabeth was able to confirm through Wickham himself, that he was never qualified to receive a position with the church. In addition to providing the bequest from his father, Mr. Darcy very fairly compensated Wickham when he chose to give up the claim to the church. Additionally, Wickham has made little effort in the subsequent years to better himself or find a profession and has gambled all his money while living a life of dissolution. He leaves behind debts, is a gamester and harms young ladies."

The three younger girls gasped with the news, but their father continued.

"Your mother and I have failed to protect you from him and, undoubtedly, other officers of less than savoury ilk. We have been negligent and concerned with our own affairs, but that will change beginning tomorrow. Kitty and Lydia, you will begin lessons with your mother to learn the sobering tasks of being a mistress of an estate."

They began to complain, but their father would not stand for it. "No, no. You are daughters of a gentleman and, thus, I wish for you to remain. I know we simply do not have many handsome bachelors who are gentlemen in our area. However, if you can make improvements in behaviour and understanding, perhaps we may all visit London for a few weeks."

"During the Season? Oh, think of the amusements!" Lydia nearly shrieked, and, although it was vulgar, Jane was pleased her primary concern was with things such as shopping instead of men. She really was too young to think of marriage.

"If you cannot control your outbursts, you shall not go and will return to the nursery."

"But, Mamma! You would not..."

Mrs. Bennet interrupted, "It is not for me to question your father's discipline, child. I wish you to do well and make a good match; you have much to learn." That was the nearest thing to reproach Jane had ever heard from her mother toward Lydia.

"Now, let us carry out our tasks for today. Girls, you shall make it quite clear to our acquaintances that Wickham has been lying about Mr. Darcy, and I will speak with the merchants."

Meryton

2:30 pm

In Meryton, Kitty and Lydia bounded into the milliner's shop, their eldest sister entering serenely behind them, and crossed to the other side of the shop. Like the other customers, they were there under the pretence of shopping but sought conversation. Lydia was not ready to condemn Wickham in her own mind, but also believed gossip harmless. In an effort to gain her father's approval, and, therefore, to enjoy London with the family, she tugged Kitty towards Mrs. Long's nieces. Before reaching them, Lydia overheard their whispers.

"Yes, Mr Smith delivered the letter himself, and collected the one from her," the elder niece said.

"But it has been said she hates him!" her sister countered.

"I believe the letters speak for themselves."

Desiring to understand whom these delicious rumours condemned, Kitty and Lydia drew closer.

"Then why did he leave?"

"To meet with the solicitor, of course!"

"So Mr. Bingley is to return? Miss Bennet's hopes shall be answered!"

"No, his proud friend will not allow him, but perhaps as sister to Mrs. Darcy, she can meet with him in Town." Only the desire for more information could restrain Lydia's impulse to shriek. As it was, she trembled in silence.

The younger niece huffed. "Well, I did not see any sign of attachment from either. How long can they have been attached?"

The elder of the young ladies drew in closer and spoke softly, causing the youngest Bennet daughters to hold their breath to hear clearly. "They say it all started when she nursed her sister who fell ill at

Netherfield, and an understanding was formed at the ball. Why else would he suddenly dance with a local lady? And then he left straightaway for Town."

At that moment Jane came to gather her sisters, and they easily agreed to leave. Lydia and Kitty raced to the rest of their family before they all left to return to Longbourn. Out of the corner of her eye Lydia thought she saw Wickham in an alley with a lady's arms about his neck, but surely he would not put his hands *there*. Briefly she felt a moment of dizziness and before she could gain a better view, Kitty pulled her towards her family.

"Mamma! Mamma!" the girls called out.

Mr. Bennet spoke instead. "Will you not heed my words from earlier? Behave like young ladies or I shall return you to the schoolroom."

"But I must tell Mamma the most ridiculous gossip we just heard in town. La! What a joke!" exclaimed Lydia.

With grave seriousness, Mr. Bennet allowed them to continue.

"Mr. Darcy has written Lizzy a letter, and she has written one back! Susanna Long was quite sure they were engaged the night of the ball! Only we know it to be impossible, for Lizzy hates him so! What a good laugh we shall have!"

Mrs. Bennet spoke sharply. "Girls! I hope you did not partake of this gossip."

"No, we had no time before Jane called us to leave," Kitty answered.

"Lizzy! Do you not agree it is the most ridiculous piece of gossip you have ever heard?" Lydia looked at her sister's pale face.

Mary spoke up. "We ought not to gossip for it displays a smallness of character and mind. There is seldom gossip without exaggeration, which at best renders the hearer gullible and at worst renders the teller malicious."

Elizabeth drew in a sharp breath of air for reasons Lydia could not understand. Before she could wonder more, Kitty was telling the family of the officers they had not been able to meet. Later, Lydia would tease her older sister for being sweet on Saunderson, but for now she wondered at the very odd behaviour of her parents and two eldest sisters.

Upon arriving home, she was walking into the drawing room when she overheard her father say to her mother, Jane, and Elizabeth: "There is nothing to stop the gossip now; however, we have seen nothing immoral or irreligious in the man. He will arrive shortly, and I have every belief he will marry Elizabeth."

Lydia could not contain her gasp, and stood there stunned. Only Elizabeth turned to look at her. Jane and Mrs. Bennet both left for their chambers, and Lydia expected Elizabeth to follow Jane. Instead, Elizabeth took Lydia by the hand and drew her to the back parlour.

"Lyddie, I know you heard Papa speaking."

"It is true? All of it? You really are engaged to Mr. Darcy?"

Elizabeth shook her head. "No, I am not engaged, but it now seems out of our hands."

"Susanna said he proposed at the ball. He did dance with you!"

"Yes, we danced, and we argued...about Mr. Wickham."

"Why are you suddenly so against him? The only thing I heard you actually accuse him of is being poor!"

"You are quite right, but I assure you Father is correct. Mr. Darcy wrote me a letter...warning me of Mr. Wickham's past."

"Mr. Darcy saw you favoured Wickham and was jealous!" Who knew Mr. Darcy could have such passionate feelings? "His letter is probably nothing more than lies!"

"Lyddie, listen to me. I was deceived by Mr. Wickham and for more than his handsome face. I believed I thought rationally, but I did not. He played on my vanity and compassion. For you, he would play on your desire for adventure. He is not alone in this world. There are many that only desire to use others."

Lydia was silent for a moment. She attempted to piece together her sister's information with the gentlemen she knew. "Like Mr. Bingley used Jane?"

Elizabeth smiled sadly. "No, dear. I do not believe Mr. Bingley intended to hurt Jane."

"How can you be so certain? Mr. Wickham is just as open and amiable as Mr. Bingley and you say one is bad and the other good?"

"Mr. Wickham was too open. He shared very private things with me about his history with Mr. Darcy, and these have been shown to be falsehoods. It was both improper and malicious. I cannot think of a single time Mr. Bingley encouraged improper behaviour. Wickham was also boasting, raising himself above Mr. Darcy. Bingley was too modest to ever do so even when it was evident to all of us he had the better disposition."

"But Mr. Darcy also raised himself above everyone!"

"Did he do so with his words? Or did we all just assign a meaning to his looks?"

"But why would Wickham lie? Gamesters cheat and are about money."

"No, gamesters are about *winning* at all costs, and he wanted to be looked upon more favourably than Mr. Darcy. And like a gamester he played us all like his cards, me more than anyone else." Elizabeth looked very saddened before she continued speaking. "Mr. Wickham enjoyed me thinking better of him than Mr. Darcy, but he has a history of seducing very young ladies. He knows exactly what to say to make the whole world fall in love with him, give him favours, and lend him money. You should not trust him at all."

Lydia huffed, but then thought of the image she saw in Meryton. Wickham was a great favourite of hers, but by no means the only officer which she admired. An alarming and serious thought formed.

"Lizzy, how am I to know if another man is like Mr. Wickham if they are all such good actors?"

Her sister laughed at that. "No, not *all* men are actors, even if they do not have an open disposition. Age and experience gives us wisdom, but more than trusting our own opinion, we should trust our father to protect us."

"But he thinks I am too silly to spend time with me!"

"Then prove to him you are not. Respect goes both ways. He will not give any to you until you respect and honour him."

Elizabeth squeezed Lydia's hand and gave her a kiss on the forehead before leaving Lydia to her suddenly serious thoughts.

Darcy carriage

4:00 pm

D arcy had grown so distraught over the idea of offending his beloved, fearing she would be forced to marry against her will, that he truly looked ill.

As they changed horses, Georgiana queried her brother.

"Now, that look I *know* is concern," she emphasized and searched his face, "and guilt. Whatever is in that letter?"

Darcy feigned ignorance.

"William, will you tell me what concerns you? If you refuse, I am afraid I will have to demand you turn it over."

Darcy stared at her in disbelief. "Mouse?" He called her by the pet name he gave her as an infant. "What has caused all this?" For months, since George Wickham broke her heart, she had been meek and shy even with him. Since learning he was to return to Netherfield she returned more to her former spirited ways.

Bingley roused at the sound of voices.

Georgiana straightened. "I am not a mouse! I am nearly grown and shall soon be out of your house. Allow me to help you."

Darcy's jaw tensed as he thought for a moment. It was true. His dear sister, whom he cared for more as a father than as a brother, was soon to come out and had already had one encounter with a villain. She had lost most of her child-like innocence due to that episode.

If I cannot protect her, at least I should respect her. And Bingley ought to know the full truth as well. For a moment the irony of the fact that he had previously held hopes for them making a match struck him. He had thought he acted brotherly to Bingley, as a stand in for his old friend Harry, but perhaps he just acted as father figure there as well.

"Very well, Georgiana. Bingley should hear this as well. I am in love with Miss Elizabeth Bennet and plan to offer for her as soon as we reach Longbourn." He was pleased to note his baby sister was not so grown that she could entirely suppress her squeal at his words. Bingley laughed, no doubt pleased with his earlier assumptions.

"But why do you seem so unsettled?"

"I..." Darcy gulped. He had severely broken with propriety and was rather hesitant to admit the truth of it to his sister, but he always found it difficult to resist anything she asked when she looked upon him with that expression.

"Elizabeth—forgive me, I cannot think of her as anything else now—is a stellar woman. I cannot explain it, but she has a combination of virtues that makes her the most amazing and fascinating young lady I have ever met. But I had not planned to propose. Her family has connections in trade, and she is nearly penniless."

Darcy rolled his eyes at the look on his sister's face. It was obvious she had been reading too many novels, for she seemed entirely unmoved by his reasonable scruples. Real life was not a fairy tale. It was natural to be prudent as to fortune, but he knew he was blessed with the independence that made the match bearable.

"But her lack of fortune and the situation of her mother's family, though objectionable, are nothing in comparison to the total want of propriety frequently and nearly uniformly betrayed by her nearest relations, except for her eldest sister."

Georgiana flushed in apparent sympathy for the young lady she had never met. "And your pride would not allow you to connect yourself with them? Honestly, Brother! Must I give you a lesson on family history? Shall I start with the *noble* Fitzwilliams? Now, which relative is your favourite? The one who seduced the youngest daughter of an earl? Or perhaps our Darcy ancestor, Marmaduke, who attempted to lead his troops entirely *bottomless* into battle, more than once, due to emptying a gin bottle the night before?"

Darcy held up his hands in protest. "Georgiana, you previously illustrated your point, and I had already begun to think differently upon the subject. But there is more..." Darcy trailed off.

Georgiana was not deficient in understanding. "If you had not *planned* to offer for her while you were in Hertfordshire, and have only just recently thought better of your reasons against the match, why are we already on the road?"

Letting out an exasperated sigh, Darcy attempted to explain. "You may have noticed I have been in poor spirits."

Georgiana rolled her eyes. "*Poor?* You have had all the geniality of a bear with a thorn in its paw." Darcy met that piece of impertinence with a grunt. *Clearly she will enjoy Elizabeth's company.*

"And Bingley as well." Bingley straightened when he heard his name.

"Yes, he has not been quite his energetic self of late." Bingley smiled at the tease, and Darcy could only shake his head in amazement.

Was it the hope of meeting Elizabeth which restored her good humour? How had he not thought it before? Georgiana did not need a marriage to a wealthy and well-connected man, she needed love and acceptance. If somehow marriage to Elizabeth damaged his position in Society, they would gain things of much greater importance.

He redirected his thoughts to the point on hand. "He has been mourning the loss of Elizabeth's eldest sister whom, he idolized. In addition to the evils against the match that I had put to him, the same as I used to suppress my own desires, I did not notice any sign of regard on Miss Bennet's side. This last was telling, and he decided to give up the lease on Netherfield so he would not be in her company again."

Georgiana chewed her bottom lip in thought. "What has changed the circumstances?"

"I now know that Miss Bennet loves Bingley." Both of his companions gasped.

"How can you possibly know that now?" They asked nearly in unison.

"Elizabeth wrote me a letter."

Georgiana's eyes went wide, and she gasped.

"I do not believe it!" Bingley nearly shouted as though Darcy had insulted a lady.

"I do not believe she meant to send it."

Georgiana scowled. Darcy saw she believed Elizabeth Bennet was nothing more than the rest of the conniving and mercenary women who hunted him.

"How can that error possibly be made?" she asked.

"I can easily understand it, for the same has happened to me. Last night my head was not as clear as usual."

"You were in your cups?" Her gaze drifted to Bingley, and he hung his head in shame.

Darcy gave her a reproachful look. "Hardly. You know I *never* over-indulge."

"According to Richard, not since that one night at Cambridge when..."

"Georgiana! Let this be a lesson to you even as that story is. I was not in my cups, but I still felt some impairment, my faculties still affected."

She snorted. "So you sent a young lady a letter?"

"No!" He was perhaps too vehement in his protest. "I only wrote one. I never meant to send it, never meant for her to read it. It was meant to be an exercise to firm my resolve and persuade me that I was right to not pursue Elizabeth. And her letter to me seemed, similarly, to be more an attempt to decipher her own conflictions over me and, obviously, was written in ignorance of my letter. She was painfully honest in stating her confused feelings, and strongly berated me on some issues; it could never be interpreted as an attempt to entice me. Neither letter, I suspect, was written in a calm, rational state, nor were they intended to be posted."

Clearly only somewhat mollified by her brother's thoughts on Elizabeth's intentions, Georgiana persisted. "Well, you did send yours, and now her reputation will be in tatters. So you are doing your duty and will marry her." She sighed. "No lady wishes to be married in such a way."

No true lady anyway, Darcy thought. He knew several who would gleefully accept him even due to scandal.

"I have my hopes that she has not read mine and may not know of it. I received an express from Mr. Bennet, so I do assume it has been received, but he may have withheld it from her."

Georgiana seemed confused by her brother's logic. "If you love her and your judgment was so impaired last night, then I suppose you said as much in your letter. Why would you wish she not know of it? She must know her letter was sent, and there is no alternative but to marry. Knowing your affection would be a reassuring balm."

Darcy grimaced. He sincerely doubted Elizabeth would find any comfort in his words. His sister saw his expression and gave him a sharp look. "What did you write?"

Darcy looked away, guilty. "Remember, I meant to save the letter to remind myself of the reasons why, no matter how great my affection, I could never marry her."

"You wrote that you disapproved of her family? Denigrated her lack of connections and dowry?"

Darcy nodded his head affirmatively. Georgiana's disgust showed on her face, but then a thought seemed to strike her. "But it is *her* letter you look at anxiously."

"Yes." Darcy said nothing more.

Georgiana looked at him in exasperation. Darcy did not doubt she was quelling the urge to lunge for the letter and read for herself. "William, do not try me today. You have insulted the lady you love and wish to marry... and now *must* marry. If you have any desire to begin your marriage in happiness, you will tell me what *her* wayward letter says."

"That she loves me against her reason and against her will, and knows nothing good of me."

Georgiana gasped. "She confessed love? Oh, William!"

"Calm yourself. She has much against me. She has surmised that I separated Bingley from her sister, who *does* love him. And..."

"But, we bring him back with us, which should ease her heart and display your honour in correcting your *very* wrong *presumption.* A lady appreciates that!"

Bingley seemed to take notice of this more than the other parts of conversation and looked quite thoughtful.

Darcy hesitated. Georgiana looked as though she might shake him until he spoke again. "And she has believed Wickham's usual lies about me."

Georgiana paled. "He-he-he...she knows him? How?"

"He has joined the Militia regiment that is quartered in Meryton."

"Has he said anything about me?"

"I do not believe so. He would know better than to risk me calling him out." Darcy's fists tightened in reflex, and Bingley's look of interest piqued.

Georgiana was quiet for a moment and Darcy looked at her in concern. "We can turn around, if you wish."

She vehemently shook her head. "No! I will no longer live in fear of him ruining my life. I once was lively. I will be myself again." She paused and looked at Mr. Bingley's confusion then straightened and held her head high. "I am ready to speak about it now. I wish to tell Mr. Bingley and then Miss Elizabeth if it should prove necessary to change her mind. You helped me and I will help you."

Darcy attempted to argue but again saw his sister would be firm in this. She succinctly told the tale and he was never more proud of her than that moment.

When she was finished Georgiana immediately resumed her questioning. "How long have you known he was there?"

"He arrived the week before I left."

"Her acquaintance with you is longer, and yet she believed Wickham."

Bingley interjected here. "Ja...Miss Bennet did ask me about Mr. Wickham at the ball. I did not know much to tell her. I believe Caroline said something as well but it was probably done in her usual, supercilious and insulting fashion. I do not believe Miss Elizabeth believed Mr. Wickham implicitly, but the man seemed very nice when I met him."

Darcy shook his head. "I did not make myself agreeable. I disliked the Bennets, and others, for their lack of decorum, and my natural reticence in crowds was seen as haughtiness. And I worry whatever feelings she has, that have withstood her disgust at my manners, will not survive the direct insult I gave in my letter."

"I assume you made it very clear you would not marry her?" Georgiana asked.

"Yes."

"She must either be very angry or entirely despairing, if she has read the letter."

"And now you know the cause for my anxiety."

Bingley was more hopeful. "Perhaps she has not read it, and only her father has."

"Elizabeth is unlikely to be alone in her criticisms of me. Mr Bennet will likely feel nearly as insulted and may refuse my offer. She is not of age."

"Most would consider you an illustrious match."

"Nothing about the Bennets adheres to a normal way of thought. She is his favourite daughter, and he often seems not to care about the components of Society that would rouse most men to take an interest in their family. If the exchange of letters is not widely known, he may not favour the match. I fear Elizabeth would refuse me should I ask her." The lack of surprise on his companions faces when he uttered his final words was telling. He would deserve it if she refused him, no matter his wealth and rank.

Georgiana broke the silence. "You do not plan to speak to her?"

"I...I have never been in the position of being less certain which path is correct. I alternately wish for the letter to be known to her, and I wish for it not to be."

"You must settle this with her. Regardless of whether the letter is known or not, nothing but entire transparency will ensure your future felicity. Anything less merely stores troubles and magnifies them."

"When did you get so wise, little mouse?" He affectionately tapped her nose. She wrinkled it but smiled at the endearment.

Bingley agreed, "Yes, you are quite wise, Georgiana. You have given me much to think on as well."

The three shared a hopeful smile as the carriage brought them closer to Meryton.

The Darcy carriage ambled into Meryton, and Darcy did not miss the sight of several townsfolk gawking at the crest. It drew even more attention than he anticipated, and he worried anew what may already be circulating. He saw the woman he believed to be Mrs. Bennet's sister flap her arms wildly about and scurry down the road to Longbourn. Bingley noticed as well and let out a strange longing-like moan.

"We do not go straight to Longbourn?" Georgiana asked.

"No. There is time for me to change at least before arriving for dinner, and you shall remain at Netherfield."

"Oh, please allow me to come!"

"You do not have an invitation and neither does Bingley, actually."

"I hardly think they would mind!" Bingley cried.

"I arrive to sort out a terrible mess and may very much be unwanted. Elizabeth wrote in her letter that she has been led to believe, by your sister no doubt, that I desire to match you with Georgiana." He ignored the looks of alarm from his friend and sister. "The family may not welcome you back so easily either. Allow me to go and do my duty and then we will see on the morrow if we may all call together."

Georgiana and Bingley let out nearly identical sighs of frustration, and Darcy rolled his eyes. His own frustration was from a different sort entirely.

An hour later he arrived at Longbourn's door in fresh clothing. The house was strangely quiet. He chose the coward's way out and requested Mr. Bennet immediately instead of greeting the ladies in the drawing room. Mr. Bennet did not seem very welcoming and chose to stare at him directly.

"Mr. Darcy, would you care to tell me your reason for visiting today?"

"I believe I owe you an apology, sir," he humbly began. "I have reason to believe a mislaid letter was sent here this morning. In it, among other things, I insulted your family."

Mr. Bennet raised an eyebrow, and Darcy had the uneasy feeling that he was the prey being played with, as a cat toys with a mouse. "And is that the extent of your travesties?"

"No, sir." He gulped. "I also declared my love for your daughter, Miss Elizabeth, and then arrogantly laid out all the reasons I chose not to offer for her. I insulted her, I blamed her for my own lack of composure, and now I worry that I have compromised her reputation."

Mr. Bennet was silent for a long time. "I believe she has sent you a letter as well. I am inclined to let the issue pass. I understand you have both exchanged admiration and insults and agree a match is nonsensical."

This was not how Darcy imagined the meeting to go. "Sir! I...you must see that there were others who handled these letters. An attachment, even an engagement, must be presumed."

"You sound very certain when you have only arrived to the area yourself, and it has been mere hours since the letters were sent."

Blast the man! He would make Darcy confess all. "I arrogantly sent notices to my solicitor and family in hopes of making it seem as though there was a pre-existing engagement. Before reading Miss Elizabeth's letter the idea that she would refuse me never occurred to me."

"Well, it is as you say. She did not think highly of your insults and might refuse you, even with what appears to be weighty proof of an engagement. It is not uncommon for ladies to think better of an attachment."

Darcy sank back in his chair. "She would harm her reputation? Even that of her sisters? The engagement would be well known, nothing so easily silenced. Does she truly think so little of me?"

He had been humbled thoroughly this day. More than this, many times now he saw that he chose a cowardly way, but now his heart demanded he be brave and fight. Not because he deserved it, but because he would not harm Elizabeth if he could help it and did not want to lose hope of her regard.

"Might I speak with Miss Elizabeth, sir? I wish to know her thoughts on this."

Mr. Bennet looked surprised, which only humbled Darcy further. The older gentleman undoubtedly did not believe Darcy was capable of following another person's wishes.

"Very well."

Mr. Bennet excused himself, and after a few moments, Elizabeth was brought in.

Darcy almost knocked over his chair when he stood at her entrance. She looked more beautiful than he recalled, but was subdued, and he would wager he saw caution in her eyes.

"You wished to speak with me, sir?"

Was she trembling? Why did he always lose his ability to speak sensibly around her? She motioned to his seat, and he obeyed her silent request.

"Mr. Darcy, I am a very selfish creature and, while it may wound your feelings for me to mention it, I must apologize for my unjust accusations in my..." she trailed off before quietly finishing, "in my letter."

"What did you say of me that I did not deserve? Even more so in light of *my* letter. I hope you have destroyed it. I wrote harshly, and it is full of expressions that should justly make you hate me."

"Please," she replied staring at her hands. "Please, do not apologize for your letter. It begins in bitterness, but the ending is so full of hopeless love."

He reached for her hands, but she pulled them away. She turned from him but said in a shaky voice, "You wrote many sensible things in the letter as well. It would be an imprudent match for you. My family's behaviour is unpardonable. I would be nothing but a blight on your family name, and I bring nothing but myself."

He stood at her words. "Elizabeth, you mean everything to me! There is nothing greater I could desire. Do not I owe it to my family to be happy?"

He had never been more ashamed of his selfishness. In his letter he sought only to ease his own feelings. Although he did not mean for her to read his thoughts on her family and connections, it was inexcusable for him to even think them. If, in the last day, he wondered if he truly loved Elizabeth he could have no more doubts. Her pain was his, all the worse for it came by his own hand.

"But would your happiness last? When your family name is diminished, your wife scorned, and your children unaccepted would you still be happy? What of your sister?"

"You are rejecting me?" This morning he felt disbelief at the notion. Now he felt only fear and knew she was every bit justified.

Her voice was low. "The feelings which hindered your earlier regard will soon allow you to overcome your pain, sir."

Darcy was silent for a long moment, desperately trying to find some kind of composure. His heart pounded and every second he was sure it would be its last beat. He circled around her, willing her to meet his eye. "And what of you, Elizabeth? Do you still find nothing to esteem in me? You wrote you love me. Are you willing to go through life without that love?"

She stared at the floor, but he saw her wipe her eyes before she faced him again to reply. "I am convinced I am the last person in the world you should marry. We both know you would not be here if not for the letters."

Panicking he declared, "But the letters are known! In an effort to affect a pre-existing engagement for us, I even sent a notice to my solicitor and my relations in London. An engagement is presumed."

Elizabeth was silent a long moment. "Your letter tells me you think little of my sense—perhaps rightly so—therefore it should come as no surprise to you that I am willing to face the consequences of either the assumption of a broken engagement or corresponding with a gentleman without one. If my family is harmed, according to your depiction, we do not have much respectability to lose. My reputation and my family is not your concern."

Colour drained from his face and he sank down into his chair. Cradling his head in his hands he knew not when Elizabeth quietly left the room. He had been allowed, encouraged, and nearly taught to be selfish and to think of none beyond his own family circle. Elizabeth could scarcely have chosen better words for her reproof. Here now was the true culmination of the plans of his life. Hope was over, entirely over. Alone with his tortured thoughts, he waited until Mr. Bennet returned.

Longbourn

5:30 pm

Mr. Bennet left his daughter and her determined suitor in the library and approached his wife's chambers again.

"Fanny," he called while knocking. "He has come."

She opened the door and her sad, red-rimmed eyes met his.

Hurrying inside and closing the door, he led her to her sofa once more. "Why do you cry?"

"What have I cost our girls? What if Lizzy does not want him, but now she must marry him because of the gossip?"

"I would not force her but I do not think you need to worry about that. Lizzy is more concerned that he will not want her."

"That man! Who is he to think he can say such things about *our daughter*? And from the very beginning!"

"Do you not see it means from the very beginning she had a profound effect on him?"

"He still thinks he is better than us. What if he resents having to marry her?"

"I do not think we need to worry about that either. When I left him I suggested he need not worry about marrying Elizabeth, and he insisted on talking to her. I believe he desperately wants to marry her. Additionally, he was quite humbled, and he worried for Lizzy's reputation. His first thoughts are for her, not himself. He has perhaps acted foolishly, but so do we all at times. I do believe he truly loves her."

"How can you be so certain, Thomas?"

"Do I not know what it is to love a woman Society said was beneath me? Did I not have to argue for our right to be together?"

"That may be, but your love faded, and my silliness did kill it. Lizzy's sharp tongue may be too much for a man with such conceit."

"You did not kill my love! I was simply selfish, thinking I saved you from bearing my presence. I pushed for our marriage, I accepted the terms of the entail." Mrs. Bennet tried to argue, but he hushed her. "We will speak more on this later. Lizzy's letter did not seem to deter him. He needs a strong wife who can set him to rights and is quick-witted enough to be his equal and to help manage his estate."

"*Her* letter! Mr. Bennet, what do you mean?"

"Elizabeth tells me that in a moment of acute distress while attempting to make out Mr. Darcy's character, she wrote him a letter and accidentally sent it. In it she admits to loving him beyond all prudent reason."

Surprisingly, Mrs. Bennet erupted in laughter. "Oh! What a good joke it is! You know I dearly love a laugh."

Mr. Bennet smiled at his wife. "Yes, and they are different from us. They do not keep things to themselves, and they begin by knowing each other's deficiencies and choosing to overcome them. But let us go downstairs. I believe we should have an announcement to make."

As Mr. and Mrs. Bennet walked hand in hand down the stairs, the letter Mrs. Bennet had been holding fluttered to the ground. They separated in the hall; Mrs. Bennet to the drawing room, and Mr. Bennet to the library, where he found Darcy alone.

"Well, son, is it all settled then?"

Darcy looked upon him with horror and misery in his eyes. "It is as you say, sir. She will not have me."

Mr. Bennet hardly knew what to think or say. In his silence, Darcy stood. "Thank you for seeing me this afternoon. I apologize, I find I cannot stay for dinner. My sister accompanied Mr. Bingley and I to Netherfield. I should see to her."

"Darcy, did Elizabeth offer you no hope?"

Darcy squeezed his eyes shut and visibly swallowed. The informal address and fatherly tone was not lost on him. Too late he realized he might have enjoyed being part of a family again. He answered the question. "She said she was completely convinced she was the last woman in the world I should marry."

"You have debated with Elizabeth enough times to know she takes advantage of degrees and professes opinions that are not her own. She did not say *you* were the last man in the world *she* would marry."

"Not this time, but she did in her letter. You did not see the turn of her countenance. There is no hope." He picked up his hat and bowed before departing.

Dinner was a very subdued affair with everyone retiring so early that supper nearly went to waste. As Mr. Bennet walked by Jane and Elizabeth's room before continuing down the hall, he heard the sound of muffled sobs and could scarcely wonder who was grieving more. He would need to have an honest discussion with his daughters on the morrow. Passing by Lydia and Kitty's room he heard more crying, which did nothing but confuse him further.

Chapter Seven

Wednesday, December 7, 1811

Longbourn

8:00 am

Elizabeth awoke early the next morning with puffy eyes. She had cried most of the night. Jane was the perfect companion. She alone could understand the feelings of rejection and lost love. It was a misery halved, but in some ways felt more acutely for Elizabeth would rather have twice the pain and Jane experience none.

She expected to be the first in the breakfast room, but found Lydia reading a letter. "I did not know the post had come already."

Lydia startled and nearly knocked over her tea. Colouring she admitted, "It is an old letter. I found it on the stairs yesterday. It is..." She did not continue and instead handed the yellowing letter with faded ink to Elizabeth who read it with wide eyes.

September 29, 1786

My Darling Fanny,

Father had me go around with the steward today to collect rents. This last week he has made me sit with the housekeeper as well. He says I will learn the thankless tasks of estate management in hopes of persuading me to find another wife. He will not succeed. I will not change my mind.

Dearest, I know Mother and Father intimidated you and made you believe you are unworthy. Who are they to know what I desire in a wife? I am their own son and they understand me little more than a stranger does.

Father has suggested the only way he will agree to our marriage is by putting an entail on the estate for one generation. He no longer trusts my sense, but when we have a son it may be broken. Which will it be? Shall we wait until we come of age, elope to Gretna Green or agree to this entail? I will abide your wishes but know that nothing you say will deter my love. I will wait for you.

Yours ever,

Thomas

"Oh, Papa. My poor mother." Elizabeth murmured through her tears. She reached for Lydia, who was crying too. They remained hugging each other until Mr. Bennet entered the room.

"What is this?" he asked with real concern. Then, seeing the letter, he picked it up before letting it drop back down to the table. "I will speak with you and your sisters after breakfast," he said with a sigh.

Before much longer the rest of the household joined them in the breakfast room. Elizabeth was struck by how quiet they all seemed. Once she would have rejoiced in the restraint. Now it was deafening.

Finally everyone finished, and Mr. Bennet invited them all to the drawing room. He silently handed the letter to Mrs. Bennet, whose eyes widened, but she said nothing.

"Girls, this is becoming quite the thing. Perhaps we will run a Salon at Longbourn." The girls all giggled.

"Well, it should come as no surprise that the most curious of our daughters have managed to find a letter I once sent your mother while we were courting."

Jane, Mary and Kitty looked curiously at their sisters, and Elizabeth calmly waited for their father's explanation.

"I know, I know. No one wants to think of their elderly parents as courting."

"Mr. Bennet!"

He smiled as he continued. "But this letter has had significant impact on us all." He took in a deep breath. "Your grandfather did not wish me to marry your mother. He believed she was beneath me, and we were both under age. At length when I proved too stubborn, he suggested an entail."

The other girls gasped. "We agreed to it, certain we would have a son to break it. With each new daughter your mother grew more anxious, and I retreated further to my library."

He took Mrs. Bennet's hand and kissed it. "We were both very worried we had made the other regret the marriage, but we never talked of it. We have only seen in the last few days the repercussions of our selfish behaviour."

This surprised Elizabeth. "But if your actions were due to concern for the other, how is that selfish?"

Mrs. Bennet answered. "Because ultimately we were more worried about our own feelings and could not face knowing our fates—if we were accepted or rejected. If we were less selfish we would have reached for each other instead of standing on our own."

Elizabeth had never heard her mother speak so sensibly, but her father was speaking again. "We were worried about the entail, which we agreed to entirely on our own. We thought we had failed you girls in what mattered most: securing the estate. We did not see that we were failing you by allowing such a disharmonious home and by neglecting your educations. I failed to practice economy and have not added to your dowries, and we have left you to your own devices to shift about as best you can. So, beginning Monday next I will have Kitty and Lydia sit with me each morning. Mary shall spend time with your mother learning more womanly arts. There shall be no balls until each of you can show me you can act sensibly."

Kitty cried out. "That is unfair! For Jane and Lizzy always have all the fun!"

"I said until each of you can show me you can act sensibly. I believe your sisters may agree they have recently failed in that regard."

Jane and Elizabeth blushed and looked to their hands. At length the others left the room and Elizabeth looked to her father.

"Papa, may I speak with you?"

"No, I believe you need your mother at such a time." He bent to kiss her on the cheek and then squeezed his wife's hand and left the room.

"Mamma?"

"Yes, my child?"

Elizabeth was silent for a moment. There could only be one thing she needed to ask her mother, but she knew not if she could face the truth.

"Mamma," she said at last. "Do you regret marrying Papa? If his family was so against you, were you treated badly? And to have your worst fears come to life!"

"Oh, Lizzy you are still so young. Look at this place. I may not get to live in it after your father passes, and it was my dearest wish for one of you girls to become the next mistress, but I have been happy here. This has been my home. But it is not the house that makes it a home. It is the love within these walls. I would not trade my daughters for any son. Your father loves me. We may not always be able to express it so well, but you can learn from my mistakes. Do not be afraid, do not be selfish, and do not hold back. That is not your way, Lizzy."

"He has told you?"

"Yes, I only know my daughter has given her heart away and is allowing it to be broken, although he offers you marriage, through your father. I wish you could have talked to me of it."

"I am sorry."

"You believed I would overthrow your wishes?" Elizabeth was silent. "I suppose you are right, but it is a mother's prerogative to believe she knows what is best for her children."

Elizabeth walked over and bent to kiss her mother's forehead. "I love you, Mamma."

"I love you, my clever Lizzy. Have no doubt, there is a way to sort this out, and you will find it. Do you believe he loves you?"

"I do. Is that enough?"

"Only you can answer that."

Elizabeth gave her mother a small smile. "I believe I will go for a walk."

She left the room, noticing Lydia had been eavesdropping in the door way. Before she had a chance to leave the house, Lady Catherine de Bourgh was announced.

"I must speak with Miss Elizabeth Bennet immediately."

Netherfield

9:00 am

Breakfast at Netherfield passed in silence. At last Bingley spoke. "What are your plans?"

Darcy did not reply. After twenty minutes passing with little more sound than the scraping of butter on toast, Bingley tried again.

"I shall inform Carver we are off again."

"No." Darcy said at last. He stood and tossed his napkin down on the table. "No. We will call on Longbourn. You desire to meet with Miss Bennet again, and Georgiana wishes to meet the ladies."

"William, I do not wish you to be uncomfortable. Mr. Bingley may go alone."

"No, I desire you to meet them as well."

"Darcy, truly you need not come. I may have decided to give Netherfield up after all. It feels right drafty this morning."

Darcy smiled a little and clapped his friend on the back. "Did you lose courage in your sleep? We have ladies to court!"

"What has gotten into you?" Bingley asked in wonder.

"A desperate resolution! Let us leave in half an hour."

Darcy grinned as he left his friend and sister in awe. Twenty minutes later he stood in the entry awaiting their presence when an express rider arrived for Darcy. He read the express with trepidation.

Wednesday, December 11, 1811

Fitzwilliam House, London

Darcy,

My mother was in the room when our uncle read your note announcing your betrothal to this Miss Elizabeth Bennet of Longbourn in Hertfordshire. Mother is now missing from Matlock House, and I am rather certain she has journeyed to Longbourn to make her complaints to the lady directly. I hope this reaches you in enough time to intervene. My best wishes to you and Miss Bennet.

Your cousin,

A. de Bourgh

Darcy immediately agreed with his cousin's opinion—his aunt must be on her way to Longbourn. He could only fear what she may say to Elizabeth and how she might insult his beloved. He realized anew that his family truly did have its share of offensiveness.

All fears regarding his reception immediately vanished, and Darcy was anxious to arrive at Longbourn. His carriage pulled up, but Bingley and Georgiana had not yet appeared. Scarcely sparing them a thought, he departed without them. His thoughts were slightly more ordered upon reaching Longbourn. He sent his carriage back to Netherfield and taking a deep breath, prepared himself to battle his aunt and woo his lady.

Longbourn

Jane sat alone in the drawing room, folding and refolding her hands, attempting to find composure. The others had gone about their usual morning pursuits. Mr. Darcy's aunt was walking with Elizabeth in the garden, and Jane had little hope the meeting would be pleasant.

Last night Elizabeth had confessed to loving Mr. Darcy and rejecting his proposal, as she was certain that his offer was made only out of duty. Elizabeth scarcely knew what would become of them all, as news of a presumed engagement was already circulating. More than sympathizing with her sister's pain, Jane could not forget that her own beloved was only three miles away, but was now unlikely to appear.

Unexpectedly, Mr. Darcy was announced.

He looked about the room and raked his hands through his hair, leaving it quite askew, before speaking quickly. "I am sorry to dispense with the normal civilities, but I was informed my aunt is here and needing...my presence."

Jane furrowed her brow as she studied him. He anxiously paced around the room while she spoke. "She is walking near the wilderness with Elizabeth." His head snapped back to Jane. Perhaps if she were a less reserved person herself she would not have noticed, but Jane saw the moment fear and desperation followed by determination entered his eyes. To her surprise, he dashed away before she could say anything else.

Elizabeth had insisted that Mr. Darcy did not truly desire to offer for her, and she was uncertain of his affections, but he looked desperate and resolved to Jane.

She thought of her parents' marriage. She always knew she never wished to marry to one of such an unequal disposition to her own, as her parents had. This morning she learned they had passionately, if imprudently, loved each other. Yet, it was not their difference in stations or dispositions that starved their love, but rather their own fears.

Jane attempted to apply that theory to her experiences. She had thought that Mr. Bingley truly cared for her, but he had quickly proved inconstant. On her side, she was too afraid to show her regard for him. Her temperament was not as open and unreserved as Elizabeth and Lydia's, and she no longer had the claims of youth as an excuse if she should make a foolish mistake and believe admiration to be more than it was. To reveal her building affection only to then be rebuffed was unthinkable. For the world to know of her disappointed dreams, the folly and vanity that she could ever think she might appeal to such a man, would be unbearable. She believed she would rather know the private pain of rejection than to be fodder for the gossips.

Or so she had always told herself. She had never fancied herself in love before meeting Mr. Bingley. Her heart was not

Letters from the Heart

lightly touched or given to extreme emotion. She generally thought well of everyone, but to truly admire and love someone was another matter entirely. Such were her thoughts when she heard a carriage pull up the drive and saw Mr. Bingley and a very pretty young lady, undoubtedly Miss Darcy, descend. She burst into tears.

While walking in the garden with Lady Catherine, Elizabeth waited for the lady to begin the explanation for her errand. She did not need to wait long.

"Yesterday I heard that you, the unknown Miss Elizabeth Bennet of Longbourn in Hertfordshire, are engaged to my nephew, Mr. Darcy!"

Elizabeth said nothing in reply.

"Surely you must contradict this falsehood being circulated!"

"If you believed it false, I wonder at you coming. How came you to hear this news?"

Lady Catherine turned red. "That matters not. I am assured of its impossibility. I insist on you answering me plainly. Are you engaged to my nephew?"

"Your ladyship has declared it to be impossible."

"Let me be clear, this match cannot take place. Mr. Darcy is engaged to my daughter."

Yesterday Elizabeth would have considered this viable, but not today. Now, she knew the honour of Mr. Darcy. She inwardly scoffed at an aunt who knew him so little. "If he is, then you should know his honour would prevent him from offering for me."

"The engagement is of a tacit nature, but every virtue forbids your match. The alliance would be a disgrace!" Lady Catherine drew closer and attempted to tower over Elizabeth. "You shall be *despised* by *everyone*."

"What care I for the favour of the world? I believe the world in general would have far too much sense to scorn my marriage to Mr. Darcy. If his family chooses to be resentful, it will not cause me one moment's concern. The wife of Mr. Darcy would have so many other extraordinary sources of happiness, she could have no regrets!"

Clearly displeased, Lady Catherine turned to increasing insults. "If you were sensible to your own good, you should not want to quit the sphere in which you have been brought up."

Elizabeth opened her mouth to retort when she heard from behind her, "I am a gentleman, she is a gentleman's daughter. We are equals."

Darcy rapidly exited the house and desperately searched for his aunt and Elizabeth. He happened upon them just as Elizabeth suggested she would be happy to marry him. He was almost too caught up in joy to hear his aunt's next words.

"If you were sensible to your own good, you should not want to quit the sphere in which you have been brought up."

Loudly and sternly he declared, "I am

a gentleman, she is a gentleman's daughter. We are equals."

Both ladies startled and turned to face him. Darcy noticed Elizabeth's heightened colour; she was furious, but became visibly relieved by his presence. *By G-d she is beautiful, even more so when angry!*

Darcy gave her a small, reassuring smile before turning his attention to his aunt, giving her his most fierce glare.

"Darcy! How can you say such a thing? Are you ignorant of the conditions of her uncles and aunts, of her mother? I know it all—her cousin is my parson and heir to this estate!"

"Whatever her connections may be, I do not object to them. They can mean nothing to you."

"You refuse to obey the claims of duty and honour?"

"No principle of either would be violated by my marriage with Miss Elizabeth."

"Nephew, I am shocked and astonished. I had thought you a reasonable young man. You desire to degrade yourself with her relations? Are the shades of Pemberley to be thus polluted? What of Anne's wealth? Does it mean nothing to you? How can you forget yourself so? I demand that you promise to never enter into a union of any kind with this woman!"

Darcy spoke clearly to Lady Catherine, but looked earnestly at Elizabeth. "I shall make no promise of any kind. I have every wish and intention of making Miss Elizabeth Bennet my wife."

Lady Catherine's eyes narrowed on Elizabeth. "I see." She pointed a finger at Elizabeth and declared menacingly, "You have drawn him in with your arts and allurements. You have made him forget, in a moment of infatuation, what he owes himself and to all of his family!"

Darcy took a step forward and caught his aunt's attention but still looked at Elizabeth. "No, aunt. I will not marry Miss Bennet due to infatuation or for any other reason than a very deep respect, admiration and love. I am not a squeamish youth. I know what I am about. I have considered this for many weeks and am certain of my course."

Elizabeth met his eyes with a softened gaze and stepped towards him, but Lady Catherine would not have it. "Miss Bennet, have you no regard for my nephew's honour and credit? You are an unfeeling, selfish girl! You are resolved then to have him?"

Darcy caught his breath and waited for Elizabeth's response.

"I have not made my sentiments plain to you before, Lady Catherine, but allow me to do so now. I love your nephew and can be persuaded to have no other husband but him."

With the last of Elizabeth's words, Darcy caught her hand in his and directed her towards a copse of trees, away from his aunt. From a distance they heard Lady Catherine shout in anger. "I take no leave of you Miss Bennet. Darcy, I am most seriously displeased!"

Darcy's and Elizabeth's eyes remained locked until the noise of Lady

Catherine receded. Elizabeth broke the silence.

"I thought you were a man of your word, Mr. Darcy," she teased. "I seem to have a written account of you vowing never to marry me because of your duty to your family."

Darcy cringed, realising she had read his words. He released her hand but countered with, "And I have one from you vowing never to marry me because you cannot esteem me."

"Yes, the words of neither are irreproachable."

"Elizabeth, do not trifle with me. My affections and wishes are unchanged, but I am no longer a coward, or puffed up by a false sense of pride. I wish, nay need, you as my wife, a wife I can love, honour and respect."

Feeling all the significance of the moment, Elizabeth reached for Darcy's hand and kissed his knuckles. "Fitzwilliam, I have already told you that you are the only man I can be persuaded to love. I now know I have every reason to respect and esteem you. What is to be done but to marry you?"

Elizabeth gasped as Darcy grinned, revealing dimples.

"My lovely Elizabeth! I know you believe me to be an arrogant and conceited man, but I must tell you the fear that has gripped my heart since I first read your letter. First it was only out of my own selfishness. I wished to marry you and was in many ways relieved I had no choice. While I quickly accepted the justness of your complaints, I considered only myself. I worried you might refuse me. As I came to consider how great the gossip might be and that you may even be *forced* to marry me against your will, I worried for your happiness. I already hated myself for making you love me against your will. Then I learned my insulting letter made you think we should not marry, that you believed I would regret our marriage and my love was just a boyish infatuation."

"Please do not blame yourself for my selfish fears."

"Selfish? No, you could never be selfish."

"Oh, but I was. I did not wish to experience your love to only be rejected later. I claimed I thought of your own feelings, but only considered mine. I was afraid, too, and yet I declare my courage always rises to every occasion."

Darcy smiled at the image. "What changed your mind?"

"I had a very enlightening conversation with my mother."

"Your mother!"

"Is it so hard to believe she has some cleverness about her? You may see little resemblance between us, but she is responsible for my upbringing."

"I...no, I do not find it so impossible. I must thank her then!"

Elizabeth laughed. "And Lady Catherine as well!"

"I will concede your mother talking with you must have been of great use, but I was in no humour to wait. Perhaps my aunt forced you to speak earlier and more passionately than you had anticipated, but it was your father who first gave me hope."

"What did he say?"

"He told me to carefully consider your words. You declared yourself the last woman in the world I ought to marry, yet you did not say I was the last man you desired to marry. After much thought, I determined that I would not give up my fight unless you irrevocably sent me away."

Elizabeth blinked back tears. "They have taught us so much."

"Perhaps, but I think a part of us understood each other by heart."

She still held his hand, and he raised his other to her cheek. His eyes dropped to her lips, and his smile dissolved into a look of tender, but fervent, need. Elizabeth could see he was waiting for some sign of encouragement, of consent, but she could never speak the words. Instead, she turned her head just enough to place a kiss on the palm of his hand that still held her cheek, and she heard him take in a sharp breath.

She looked into his eyes as he leaned in closer. "Elizabeth," he said reverently. He was so close she could feel his breath on her cheek, causing her eyes to flutter. He moved his other hand to her face, and now cradled it in his large hands as she held her breath.

"Elizabeth." His voice was low and hoarse. He looked at her lips again. "May I kiss you?"

Slowly he leaned his head still closer, his lips so near that the smallest nod of her head or murmur of assent would make their lips meet. She gave just the briefest tilt of her head, and he pulled her even closer.

Darcy very softly and tenderly brushed his lips against Elizabeth's. Instantly, he was addicted. He needed another kiss, and another, and another. They were slow and tentative at first, as he did not wish to frighten her. In truth, he could not help himself. Her kisses were so innocent, so sweet, and she was beginning to respond eagerly to his persistence.

He drew in her top lip, and she further opened her mouth to him. He stifled a groan at just the hint of moisture on her lips, tantalizing him. Although she made no indication she desired to stop or leave, he found himself gently holding her in place with his hands. His thumbs stroked her silky cheeks. Somehow, through the haze and joy of feeling Elizabeth's increasing passion, he realized he needed to restrain himself.

Darcy pulled back and was pleased to hear her breathing was ragged and to see that her face was flushed and eyes were darkened with desire. He could not curb his passion - *just one more kiss,* he told himself. After his last peck, which made Elizabeth giggle in delight, he looped her arm through his and began to pull her towards the house.

Chapter Eight

Wednesday, December 11, 1811

Longbourn

Jane sat in the drawing room, nervously twisting her handkerchief. She continually wiped her eyes, but the streams of tears would not cease. If being a Bennet taught her anything, it was to behave as though nothing was amiss. Her every intention was to act as though all was well, even if her face was tear-streaked as she spoke to Mr. Bingley and Miss Darcy.

Instead of Mr. Bingley being shown in, it was Miss Darcy alone who was brought in and announced by Mrs. Hill.

"Miss Bennet," Georgiana said. "Mr. Bingley wished me to give you this letter. He said he would be in the side garden if you wished to speak with him after reading it."

Jane took the letter with shaking fingers but could not speak.

"I understand my brother is speaking with Miss Elizabeth somewhere?" She sounded hopeful, and Jane was pleased to understand that Darcy did not mean to give up on Elizabeth so easily. Jane only nodded her head.

Georgiana awkwardly stood for another minute, as though she had more to say, but then curtsied and left to Jane knew not where. In any other situation she would be aggrieved at her poor hostessing skills, but today she did not care.

Tearing open the seal, she found a very neatly written letter. Clearly Mr. Bingley had put much effort into writing it.

Wednesday, December 11, 1811

Netherfield Park

My dearest Angel, My darling Jane,

When Darcy suggested I return to Netherfield Park, I was at once elated even as fear gripped my heart.

I must confess there was a mismanagement in my education and, even if there was not, I was not raised to be the heir. My elder brother died unexpectedly four years ago, and Darcy took me under his wing. Being ill-prepared, I have been ever afraid of making mistakes and shaming my family legacy, and I have been diffident in grasping the responsibilities left to me.

This same cowardliness led me to delay returning to Hertfordshire to discover the sentiments of your heart. Not only are the obligations of a married man a daunting thought, I had a very real fear that you did not care for me at all, as much as we appeared to enjoy each other's company. I had wished to avoid direct knowledge of my rejection by courting your good opinion. I persuaded myself that you did not care for me, with no word from you on the matter, because of my selfish pride and fears.

I can finally admit the truth which has terrified me. I love you deeply. I may have thought myself infatuated with other ladies before, but, when worried of the lady's indifference, I found I never cared enough to seek the truth. With you, I must know. You must tell me. I know you are truly kind and would never wish to pain me, and so I have written this letter rather than importune you with my presence. If you care for me at all, and are prepared to give me a chance to prove my worth, you may find me in the garden we first walked in. If you do not appear, I will know by your silence. I dare not have hope, but at last I have courage.

I will only add,

God bless you,

Charles Bingley

Jane could scarcely think straight. That Bingley truly did love her, but was in so much doubt as to her returned affections, was hard to credit. Had she truly hidden her feelings so much? He was nearly convinced of her indifference!

His disappearance had hurt her badly. Jane realized now, Caroline had plotted to kill Jane's love for Bingley, to cause her to give up her hopes; had his sister also sought to discourage him? Had she truly any right to such hopes, Jane wondered, when she had not encouraged Bingley enough? When, out of her own selfish fear, she allowed him to feel such misery? No! It must not be! She fled the room.

Lydia lurked in the hallway outside the drawing room. It was how she always gleaned gossip. Already this morning she learned Elizabeth was in love with Mr. Darcy but had refused his offer of marriage. Now, his sister was in her very home. She pressed her ear against the door to hear the conversation in the drawing room when the door unexpectedly opened, and Lydia nearly fell on top of Miss Darcy.

"I beg your pardon," Georgiana meekly whispered.

Lydia sniffed but allowed Georgiana to entirely exit the room and close the door.

"So you're Miss Darcy? I have heard a lot about you."

Georgiana coloured, and Lydia smiled.

"Yes, you should blush. I have heard you were too proud to marry Mr. Wickham and scandalously broke off your engagement with him!"

Georgiana sharply looked up. She looked as though she might cry but then shook her head and squared her shoulders.

"Is there some place we might talk in private, Miss...?"

"I am Lydia Bennet."

"Is there some place we might talk in private, Miss Lydia?"

Lydia considered for a moment, but then decided it was just as well to speak with one of Mr. Darcy's relations when another one was out of doors with Elizabeth and his best friend was wandering around in the garden. How odd it was for Longbourn to be so besieged by people of such pride and wealth!

"This way." She scurried off and did not even glance back to see if she was followed. Lydia led Georgiana to the old school room. They now used it for large projects, such as modifying gowns for balls.

"Miss Lydia," Georgiana began with all the authority of her elder brother, though it was hardly the thing that would work on Lydia. "I do not know what specifically Mr. Wickham has explained to you about the circumstances, but I know his failures have been explained by my brother to both your father and elder sister."

Lydia huffed. "Yes, they both declare Wickham is a gamester and has seduced women. But what is this compared to true love?"

"Oh, and you think you are in love with him?"

"Every girl in the area is out of their senses about him. Lizzy included! Your brother can only have a chance with her by blackening Wickham's name, and Lizzy believed him readily enough due to his money, I dare say."

Georgiana scoffed. "You truly believe this? Your sister *loves* my brother! She even wrote of it in a letter!"

This was the first time Lydia had heard that Elizabeth loved Mr. Darcy, let alone the shocking news that Elizabeth broke with propriety and wrote him a letter. She feigned her calm. "Everyone must have some money to live on; the handsome as well as the plain, the agreeable as well as the disagreeable and spiteful, hateful, haughty creatures."

"You mean to insult my brother? He is here now declaring his love once more, and I believe we will soon be family."

"The whole neighbourhood hates him!"

Lydia would have imagined herself in a complete triumph over her companion if Miss Darcy had not turned so red, this time in anger. Lydia did not wonder at the reaction, she had intended to provoke and was pleased to see some youthful spirit emerge from the elegantly dressed lady she had heard was too proud to speak.

"You know nothing of what you speak! My brother *saved* me from Mr. Wickham's evil schemes. Last summer I nearly *eloped* with him, without informing my brother. Nor would I have had the protection of a wedding settlement, which was his entire goal. I am to inherit thirty thousand pounds and Mr. Wickham, who we have since discovered had a prior acquaintance with my governess at the time, convinced her to take me to Ramsgate for a holiday. There he declared his love for me and I was run away with the romance and delighted in the attention.

"When William arrived unexpectedly, I happily told him my news. I have never seen my brother so displeased! Mr. Wickham hastily left, never to return. My brother wrote him a letter warning him off and Mr. Wickham only replied 'The stupid cow is not worth your damned thirty thousand.'"

She paused and Lydia perceived some tears welling in Miss Darcy's eyes but they seemed more from anger than pain.

Taking a deep breath Georgiana continued, "I know not how he has lived since leaving Ramsgate, but I am certain he has done nothing but search for some new heiress to seduce. But with a man so unscrupulous as that, you cannot expect him to genuinely have feelings for a single mortal other than himself. If I had married him, I am certain I would have been left in poverty as he gambled away my fortune. If Mr. Wickham loved anyone other than himself, where is his courage to fight for it?"

Lydia collapsed onto a chair. She hardly gave credence to Miss Darcy's words alone, but when combined with the words of her parents and sisters, as well as what she believed she saw in Meryton, Lydia's beliefs were finally shaken, and she began to see clearly. She had deliberately flaunted propriety out of fear of being found unacceptable. If she knew the looks of dislike she got were either due to disgust at her manners or jealousy at her liveliness, then she need not fear she was disliked for herself and some innate quality within her.

She could never be as beautiful and sweet as Jane nor as clever and witty as Elizabeth. Mary worked diligently for accomplishments, and Kitty at least was amiable and pliable. Lydia could find no other way to recommend herself but through wildness. And yet, what did casting off propriety nearly gain the young girl in front of her? Lydia had no older and wiser brother to take an interest in her life and save her from scoundrels. She was spoilt by her parents and her sisters, though attempting to guide her, often ignored her.

What would Wickham, or any man, want with her? Georgiana at least had a fortune. Lydia had read enough novels to finally understand her danger. She would have had no means to induce such a man to matrimony and would have been left ruined with no means for support but through her own self.

Lydia stood and intended to speak but, feeling the full effects of having inherited her mother's nerves, she fainted in a heap, leaving Georgiana to sound the alarm.

Bingley paced up and down the small garden to the right of Longbourn. On the second story was a window through which he thought he had first glimpsed Jane on the day he returned Mr. Bennet's call in early October. A little over a week later, he walked with Jane in this garden before the dinner to which the Netherfield Party had been invited. That day he had felt only happiness. When he danced with Jane, he believed her an angel, and every minute in her presence continued to confirm his belief. Now, eight weeks later, and after nearly two weeks of separation from her, he came to believe more in her humanity than ever before. While he had been so busy worrying over *her* acceptance of *him*, he never considered how *she* felt about his actions. Had he wounded his beloved angel?

A movement caught his eye, and Jane darted into view.

"Mr. Bingley," she said without hesitation, and Bingley held his breath.

"Mr. Bingley, you sir, are a blind idiot! The whole county knows I am in love with you!"

Her tone was nothing like he ever expected her to use, but then her words were nothing like he ever expected to hear.

"You love me?"

"Yes!" she said with enthusiasm. "Yes!

I love you!"

She began to laugh freely, and Bingley joined in, grabbing her hands.

"I love you, darling!" Feeling uncommonly giddy, he stooped down and kissed her soundly on the lips.

"Ohh!" she cried in surprise.

Although blushing, she did not break her gaze with him and he was tempted to kiss her anew. Attempting to redirect his thoughts he thought seriously on her previous words. "Everyone knows you love me? Have they been awful to you while I have been away?"

She hung her head low. "No, not awful."

He gently tilted her head up. "Oh, Jane. You are too kind. How terrible I have been to make you doubt me."

"You are here now."

"I am! And so are you! But how can you forgive me?"

"Did I not cause you misery, too?"

"No, no, the fault was all my own. I

assumed your feelings and without even telling you mine. What were you to do?"

"Well, I...I could have written a letter?"

Her words sent them both into laughter. It might have been followed by an awkward silence but Jane seemed determined to continue to speak her mind.

"But...but...I need more time. I believe we both have the courage to declare our feelings, but one letter cannot erase our distrust."

"A courtship then?" Bingley cautiously put forth. "As it should have been weeks ago?"

Her relief was obvious and she agreed with eagerness. "Yes, that is exactly what I would wish."

Bingley leaned in for another kiss when suddenly Georgiana was running from the door and crying in alarm for help.

Darcy, Elizabeth, Bingley and Jane all arrived at the door to Longbourn as one.

"What is it?" Darcy demanded of Georgiana.

She could only stutter out, "M-m-miss Lydia!"

"Where?" cried Elizabeth.

Georgiana pointed to the old school room door, and the group pushed forward. Jane took Georgiana aside and gently helped her sit.

"Miss Darcy, are you well? You look terribly pale."

"I am very frightened. She just collapsed!"

Lydia did not rouse, and Darcy and Bingley, mindful of her head, carried her to the sofa in the drawing room, the others trailing behind.

"I will call Hill and my parents," Elizabeth said while pulling the cord.

The servant arrived in a moment and was clearly alarmed at the sight.

"Hill, please ask my parents to attend promptly and fetch Mamma's smelling salts."

Darcy was pacing around the room when Mr. and Mrs. Bennet entered.

"What has happened?" Mr. Bennet asked.

"Lydia fainted, only she will not wake," Jane said.

By this time the commotion of the house was so great that Mary and Kitty entered the room as well.

"Thomas! What are we to do?" Mrs. Bennet was growing alarmed.

Darcy approached, "Excuse me, sir, but I think it best to send for the apothecary immediately, and I will send for my physician from Town."

Mr. Bennet looked at him for a long moment. He was too reserved of a man to say much, but Darcy saw the usual laughing glint in his eye disappear and be replaced with concern. "You think this serious; have you seen this before?"

Darcy slowly nodded and spoke quietly. Only Mr. Bennet and Elizabeth could hear. "My mother. She had an acute sickness strike her. See how Miss Lydia perspires and her breathing is so shallow? My concerns may be for naught, but I think she ought to be moved to a sick bed."

"I will ready things," Elizabeth offered.

Darcy managed a very small smile when he saw Elizabeth rise to the occasion. How did he ever think she would be incapable of managing manage his homes? Georgiana was still distressed and Miss Kitty facilitated between believing Lydia was getting too much attention and wailing her best friend's unknown condition. Jane and Miss Mary went after Elizabeth to help and despite the noise of Kitty, Darcy recognized it was quieter than he expected.

Scanning the room again, he recognized Mrs. Bennet standing over Lydia, who still lay on the sofa. She gently stroked her daughter's hair. She was entirely silent but tears streamed freely down her face. Mr. Bennet wrapped one arm around his wife and was murmuring something in her ear. The tenderness surprised Darcy and he turned away from intruding on their private moment. He turned his attention to Bingley and they considered the best way to transport Lydia upstairs to the chamber when it was ready.

An hour later, Mr. Jones arrived and examined Lydia.

"It is as Mr. Darcy feared. I have bled her, but I believe this illness is beyond my experience. It is good a physician has been sent for. In the meantime, I must ask that those who are not family leave immediately," he told the assembled group.

Jane began to cry, and Bingley was at her side instantly. "I will not leave you again, Jane."

"No! I could not bear it if you became ill, too."

Darcy interjected, "My friend and I assisted in moving Miss Lydia several times now, and my sister was alone with her when she fainted. I doubt the wisdom of us now leaving."

"It is all my fault!" Georgiana wailed. "She would not believe me about Mr. Wickham, and I was too forceful!"

Everyone hastened to tell her that could not be the case, and Elizabeth attempted to console her. When the apothecary amended his statements that everyone should stay confined to Longbourn, Elizabeth took the sobbing Georgiana to her room.

A storm began, delaying the physician until morning. The house was still and sombre, the various ladies of the house were reduced to mostly silent tears. They all retired early and the situation was grave enough Darcy managed to give little thought to the fact that he was once again only a few doors down from a sleeping Elizabeth.

The next morning arrived with dark clouds in the sky, though the roads proved passable for the physician. He scarcely had more information to give but he did have additional medications to try. They had little effect. Lydia lay abed insensible to everything, with a high fever and symptoms of delirium.

Elizabeth, Jane and Mrs. Bennet took turns remaining at Lydia's side. The gentlemen consoled the ladies as best they could. Mary and Kitty took to keeping Georgiana occupied. Elizabeth had scarcely been able to comfort her. Georgiana still blamed herself entirely.

On the second night of Lydia's illness even Elizabeth's spirits began to slip. Darcy sat with her hand in hand next to Lydia's bedside. The door was open for propriety although it was unnecessary. Elizabeth wiped her sister's brow and in what Darcy believed was a fit of exhaustion began to weep uncontrollably. He pulled her to his chest and pressed kisses in to her hair until she calmed. Then she looked up to him with reddened eyes.

"I never gave her enough attention. I was content to merely scold or laugh at her. And now..."

"No, Elizabeth. I will not allow you to despair. I have seen the deathbed. Look, her cheeks are still rosy."

She looked more hopeful but still did not quite believe him. "But you said your mother..."

"Lydia is stout and young. My mother was always frail. Nor does Lydia cough. The physician tells us not to fear yet."

She laid her head against his shoulder again and said, "I will try."

"Dearest, you are a very affectionate sister. Would you still have come to Netherfield if it was Lydia who was sick instead of Jane?"

"Of course!" She wrapped her arms around his waist. "I am so thankful you are here with me."

Regardless of being able to assuage Elizabeth's feelings of guilt, Darcy recalled her words from only a few days ago. The Bennets were soon to be his family and were now on the brink of tragedy but he should have felt for their concerns long ago. Maybe they never had a daughter facing an illness before, but they had always been worthy of his notice. From his first acquaintance with them they had welcomed him into their home. It was only after his poor behaviour that Mrs. Bennet felt compelled to publically reprimand him at Netherfield. At the time he was angry at Mrs. Bennet, first for insulting himself and secondly for embarrassing Elizabeth but he had brought it on himself entirely.

When he would join Mr. Bennet in the library, the older gentleman was full of recriminations as well. The sensible people in the household knew Lydia's illness was not caused by Georgiana's revelation of Wickham's true nature but as the physician offered little hope or information, it was impossible not to have regrets. Darcy did admire the way the family came together, though. He had not experienced that kind of unity and acceptance—of being able to show weakness and have others provide support—in a very long time. He only hoped it did not come too late.

Saturday, December 14, 1811

Elizabeth stretched her back after sitting watch over Lydia. Jane was taking her place, and Elizabeth determined she must speak with her future sister.

Entering the small music room she asked Mary and Kitty to leave her alone with Georgiana, who immediately cast her eyes down.

"Miss Darcy, are you feeling well?"

"Yes, only I still hate myself for making Miss Lydia collapse. I can hardly believe I spoke so forcefully. You must despise me!"

Elizabeth sat next to her on the pianoforte bench. "Why would I despise you?"

"I have been so foolish! I know my brother informed you of my near elopement with Mr. Wickham. Then I stormed into your home and berated your sister when she certainly was not so stupid as I. It was nothing but selfishness and pride! I was ready to explain matters to you but I did not wish to appear so ridiculous to her after she insulted me and William. Mr. Wickham is terrible, but I share much of the blame and I did not wish to say that to your sister."

"I assure you, Lydia needed to hear it and not in gentleness. She has been spoiled by my parents. My mother indulges her and my father only wishes to silence her pleas for trinkets and money. She needs a strong hand. How curious that she got it from you, who, I understand from your brother, had been feeling exceptionally meek of late. I think it very brave of you!"

"Brave? It is not as though I fought on a battlefield."

"No, but that is not the lot we women have. Our power is so limited, but we must wield it with assuredness and with spirit. We may only have voices instead of weapons of warfare, but it does not make them any less important. Speaking to Lydia so forcefully was not the first time you were so courageous either. Your brother has told me how helpful you were on his journey to Longbourn and that you admitted to the premeditated elopement yourself. You risked displeasing him in both instances but stood for the truth."

"I...I did not think of it that way."

"Well, I think we seldom realize we are so brave in the midst of the battle. At the time it only appears necessary."

"Thank you, Miss Elizabeth. I am so thankful you forgave William and agreed to marry him!"

"Your brother had much to forgive me of as well. Did you ever realize forgiveness requires bravery?"

"How so?"

"It can be terrifying to let go of your feelings and face a new world. This is true not only when forgiving a person—of not holding a grudge—but in forgiving *yourself.* I know I certainly am having a time of it when I think of how terribly I treated your brother."

"But he insists you are innocent of all wrongdoing!"

Elizabeth smiled. "Your brother is a very generous man. No, I was wrong to be so prejudiced and to allow my vanity and pride to be hurt. To speak so freely against him and I was especially wrong to hurt him so badly by refusing his suit. He was willing to give up so much for me and all I could think of was myself! I was terrified of giving up my life at Longbourn and facing a world that may not accept me. I was afraid of what my life would be like if your brother ever changed his affections." Elizabeth wiped a few tears from her eyes.

"But William is the most loyal gentleman! There is nothing you could do to destroy his love!"

"I know, dear. And I am grateful for it. So you see, it was nothing about *him* and all about *me*. But I must learn to admit to my errors without losing my self-respect. I was foolish but it is not unforgiveable. It is only a lesson."

"I am so glad you are to be my sister! Maybe...maybe we could talk about this again?"

"I would like that. And since we are to

be sisters, first you must call me Lizzy and secondly, you must know sisters are not always so sensible or so dull. Come, let us learn a silly duet to cheer the family with as we wait for Lydia to recover."

Georgiana smiled, and Elizabeth breathed a sigh of relief. It had taken two days for Georgiana to overcome her shyness and speak more than a monosyllable to any of the Bennets once the apothecary pronounced Lydia seriously ill. Georgiana was even more reticent with Elizabeth than the others, leading Elizabeth to believe Georgiana genuinely disliked her. What sister could not hate a woman who abused her beloved brother so abominably in a letter? Elizabeth had been ashamed of that letter as soon as she realized it was sent but after this conversation, she would look on the past only as it gave her pleasure. More than a common interest in music, and any other topic she would later speak on with her future sister-in-law, Elizabeth discovered that she and the Darcys could teach each other a few things about forgiveness and bravery.

Monday, December 16, 1811

Longbourn

N o one else in the household fell ill, and eventually the guests were given permission to leave Longbourn. Despite the fact that the Darcys and Bingley could now remove to Netherfield, they preferred to stay at Longbourn until more was known. In the meantime, gossip had made its way through Meryton, and on the fifth day of Lydia's illness visitors began to arrive.

Lady Lucas sat in the parlour with Jane, Elizabeth, Darcy and Bingley. Mrs. Bennet was too nervous for visitors, and the younger girls were reading in a different room.

"Are there no signs of Miss Lydia's improvement, then?" Lady Lucas indelicately asked. "Your father—that is the rest of the family—is well?"

Jane replied as civilly as possible, "Dr. Coyle is very hopeful she will make a full recovery soon, and the rest of us are entirely healthy."

"Such excellent news!" After an awkward pause, she continued. "Eliza, we were so surprised to hear of your engagement to Mr. Darcy."

"Why should you be? Mr. Darcy is the most honourable and generous gentleman. He is the one who determined Lydia needed a physician and sent for his own." She took Darcy's hand in hers and squeezed it tightly.

Lady Lucas watched in fascination, then turned to Jane. "And we were so pleased to hear of Mr. Bingley's return! They do say one wedding brings on another."

Bingley attempted to speak, but Jane interrupted. "It seems you are very well informed, Lady Lucas."

"So you are engaged then?" Her incredulous exclamation was horribly insensitive for the nature of her call.

Bingley again tried to speak, but Jane blushed and said, "My mother's fondest wishes are coming to fruition. Yes, she has two daughters to be married."

Lady Lucas was silent for a moment, looking quite envious, before she turned the conversation. "Mr. Darcy, I am so happy to learn the dreadful rumours Mr. Wickham was spreading are untrue. I am even happier the scoundrel left the area when he learned he was the cause for Miss Lydia's illness."

The group collectively gasped and looked at each other in wonder.

"I have not the pleasure of understanding you, madam," Elizabeth said.

"Mr. Jones has said when Miss Lydia learned the truth of Wickham's character she collapsed and fell ill. Why of course realizing his lies was too much for a young lady of breeding such as Lydia to countenance! Such unscrupulous and terrible young men attempting to pass themselves off as gentlemen these days!"

The others said nothing, and Lady Lucas looked at her watch. "Well, do greet your parents for me, dear Jane and Eliza. It was a pleasure meeting with you, and congratulations again on your engagements to such fine men. Charlotte was so happy to hear her two dearest friends are to be so well settled," she dropped her voice, "especially if this malady does not soon quit your family, and you must leave Longbourn."

The four could only give tight smiles and nod their heads. Elizabeth escorted Lady Lucas to the door, while Darcy left to request a horse be readied. Jane and Bingley sat alone in the drawing room.

"Jane! You declared to Lady Lucas that we are engaged to be married!"

She blushed, all her boldness gone. "Yes."

"Why, dearest? You had said you needed more time to trust me."

"I have had time to trust you. You have scarcely left my side. I know my feelings, and you know yours. Neither of us have reason to doubt again."

He gathered her hands. "You are certain you wish for this?"

"Yes, Charles. I have wished to be your wife for many weeks now. Your leaving was only a misunderstanding, but, after I knew your feelings, I still worried for your constancy out of my own fears. I finally have courage, too. I love you."

Such a declaration could only be met with delight on Bingley's side and, after exchanging whispered and fervent words of love, he left to ask for Mr. Bennet's blessing.

Darcy and Elizabeth met in the hall, returning from their errands.

"Dearest, I must go to Meryton. I fear Wickham has left debts behind."

Elizabeth eyed him uneasily. "That is all you mean to do? You know, of course, he was not the cause for Lydia's illness."

"What do you imagine I would do? Attempt to chase him down and duel him? No, I believe I have seen the last of George Wickham. He knows how upset I was after his designs on Georgiana. If *he* believes it possible for me to think he was the cause for my future sister's condition then he knows to run and never see my face again."

Elizabeth thought this over and searched Darcy's face for the truth. "Yet still you must go and do the honourable thing to clear his name. Where is your implacable resentment?" She tugged on the lapels of his coat.

"If he will truly leave me alone now, then I can certainly forgive him of anything, but I do this to honour my father...and..."

"And?"

"And for you."

"Me!"

"It will distress you if your neighbours are harmed by Wickham, even if it is by his absence. I was shamed more than I could say when, in your *second* refusal to marry me, you said you and your family were not my concern. I was taught to think meanly of the rest of the world's sense and worth, to care only for my own family. I do believe, however, even if we were not engaged to marry I would have done everything in my power to help Lydia and, if I knew of Wickham leaving debts, I would settle them."

"I am sure you would," Elizabeth then smiled and kissed him gently. Darcy reluctantly pulled away to leave on his errand, and Elizabeth returned to Jane in the drawing room to wait on the arrival of the physician.

Lydia began to awake as a vile liquid was poured down her throat. Choking and sputtering, she opened her eyes to see a strange man staring down at her, and her mother sobbing and exclaiming in joy.

Soon there was a pounding on the stairs and the whole household, including Mr. Bingley and Miss Darcy, flooded into her small room. Her eyes searched for Mr. Darcy—she must speak with him!

As it happened, she was too weak to speak at all. She was made to sip some broth, although her throat ached. The well-wishers were soon pushed out of the room and only her father and mother remained.

Mr. Bennet hugged her side. "Lyddie, Lyddie. We are so happy you are awake!"

"Lydia, my baby. You must never be ill again! To frighten your poor Mamma in such a way!"

Mrs. Bennet's words were not the shrill tone she expected.

"You did this to get out of your reading, did you not? And threw the whole household, even the whole neighbourhood out of sorts! You ran off Mr. Wickham when even your mother's gossip did not work."

It was absolutely necessary to speak now. "M-m-m-mr. Darcy?"

Mrs. Bennet squeezed her daughter's hand. "He is on an errand in Meryton. Do you wish to speak with him when he returns?"

She could only nod her head. They stayed another few minutes, but she had been given medicine to sleep and soon her eyes closed.

When she next awoke, she saw Elizabeth sitting next to her.

"Lydia, here darling, drink some tea." Lydia was grateful for the assistance and the liquid. Before her illness she would have been pleased with the attention, but now she only felt shame.

"Lydia, did you still wish to speak with Mr. Darcy?"

Lydia looked around the room, expecting to see him. When she did not see him then, momentarily, she felt fear; he did not wish to see her after how cruel she had been! However, Elizabeth spoke without waiting for an answer.

"I will bring him in. He usually sits in here with me, but is just speaking with Papa."

Elizabeth squeezed her hand and left to find Darcy. Lydia relaxed, but could not be at ease.

Soon Mr. Darcy appeared in the doorway.

"Miss Lydia! It is a pleasure to see you awake and looking so well. I regret I was away earlier."

Elizabeth asked him to sit, and they both waited for Lydia to speak, but she found it difficult to find the words.

"Lyddie, would you like more rest first?"

"No, Lizzy. I must speak now." She took a deep breath and looked at Darcy before speaking in a hoarse voice. "Mr. Darcy, I must apologize to you and your sister. Regardless of how many times I was informed that Mr. Wickham said nothing but lies about you, I persisted in thinking he the better man. I called you names and unjustly accused you, even to your sister's face, even after I learned you loved Lizzy. I never questioned how such a supposedly-terrible man could love Lizzy. How could such a terrible man be capable of the passion and sacrifice I heard of you? But the only good we knew of Wickham came from his mouth. Mr. Bingley, at least, liked you. Will you forgive me for being an ignorant, silly and vain creature?"

Lydia was crying and could not quite credit what she heard next.

"Of course I forgive you, Miss Lydia. Can you forgive me for thinking myself superior to you and your family? Georgiana told me of her conversation with you. No, no keep your apology. You see, my sister has folly in her as well. My aunt came and horribly insulted Elizabeth and your family, full of arrogance, prejudice and greed, intent on matching me with my cousin. I, too, was prejudiced and full of pride, but I now very much look forward to calling you sister."

"Sister? Truly?" She looked to Elizabeth.

"Yes, it has all been settled for many days. Now you must get better so we may host a dinner to celebrate our engagement and Jane's as well."

"Jane and Mr. Bingley? How wonderful!" she exclaimed with a hint of her usual enthusiasm. Then she sank back against her pillow. "How exhausting."

Darcy and Elizabeth laughed, then left, allowing Lydia to recover.

Tuesday, December 17, 1811

Kitty came into the drawing room, where the entire household was gathered, bearing a stack of letters. The Darcys and Bingley had yet to remove to Netherfield, although they were to leave that evening. Lydia was downstairs for a few moments to take in some fresh air.

"Goodness! Have we received a letter from every acquaintance we have ever had?" Mrs. Bennet excitedly declared.

Kitty dutifully passed-out the letters and each person opened their letter in as secluded a position as possible.

Mrs. Bennet opened her letter and leaned toward the light shining through the window. She had all but forgotten about the express she sent to her sister-in-law on the day Darcy arrived at Longbourn.

Fanny,

Truly you ought to be ashamed of the way you scared me by sending your latest letter express. I found it hard to believe Elizabeth engaged to Mr. Darcy, as in her most recent letter she decries him as hateful and arrogant and we know he is vastly superior in rank and wealth. Yet, London is ripe with rumours of their engagement. I took the liberty of writing some former acquaintances of mine who remain in the Lambton area, near Pemberley, in Derbyshire. Their replies are full of nothing but glowing reports of his character. They do assume he has some pride, but pride he must either have, or the people of a small market town which he does not visit frequently, would assume he does. His rumoured wealth is well over ten thousand pounds per annum, as well as vast holdings. I asked after Mr. Wickham as well, who is not to be trusted and, when he departed the Lambton area, he left behind many debts, settled by Mr. Darcy.

But pray, write to me immediately and let me know how this engagement has come to pass. I cannot fathom Lizzy marrying a man simply for his wealth and by all accounts Mr. Darcy is too sensible to be taken in by infatuation.

Yours,

M. Gardiner

Elizabeth sat beside Darcy on the sofa and began to blush at the opening lines of her aunt's letter.

My Dear Niece,

Are you out of your senses to marry this man? Have you not always hated him? You have said he is a proud, disagreeable man, but that would be nothing if now you truly liked him; please assure me your motives are pure.

I believe that some of your opinions were based on the claims of Mr. Wickham. However, I have heard from my Lambton friends that Mr. Darcy is a generous landlord and master, and that Wickham is a gamester and philanderer, and left the area in debt. Instead, it appears that Mr. Darcy may be a good man, based on these reports, but this alone is not a sufficient basis for a marriage.

I cannot think you so mercenary to marry Mr. Darcy if you hated him, so I suppose you have learned he is not unscrupulous as you had previously believed him but your lively talents place you in the greatest danger in an unequal marriage. You must esteem your husband to escape discredit and misery. You must respect your partner in life. I suppose you are concerned as your mother had hopes of matching Jane with Mr. Bingley, who I understand has left the area, and perhaps you feel guilty after rejecting Mr. Collins, but you must not marry without affection!

However, I know not how you could break such a well-known engagement without serious consequences, for all of London is speaking of it, but if you should think better of it and need distance from Longbourn know that you are always welcome with us. I will be at Longbourn in two days and you must tell me all then!

Yours,

M. Gardiner

Mr. Bennet stood before the fireplace while reading his brother-in-law's note, wavering between offense and amusement.

Bennet,

My wife had the most distressing

letter from my sister and has informed me there is much gossip that Lizzy is to marry Mr. Darcy of Pemberley. We know this cannot be as Elizabeth hates him, and why should he care for her? Even still, it seems we are to be the victims of cruel gossip, and I know not what is to become of the family if we cannot persuade Mr. Darcy to marry her. I know you do not wish to hear it, but if it would help I can offer to settle some money on her to entice Mr. Darcy, although I could not match what many eager debutantes could provide. As you are such a poor correspondent, I have arranged my business so Margaret and I can leave earlier than usual for our annual visit. We will arrive in two days time.

Yours,

E. Gardiner

Darcy sat next to Elizabeth and noticed while she opened her letter in happiness and seemed to sink into confusion, he viewed his message with scepticism. He had heard Lady Catherine's opinion of his marriage, now he was to learn the opinion of his uncle, a powerful earl.

Darcy,

You have not replied to my message from last week so I visited your house and learned you were in Hertfordshire, and only urgent notices were being forwarded. Why on earth have you not returned to London? Your cousins and my wife are gladly, nay eagerly, relating the details of your engagement, of which I believe there is a fair amount of fabrication. Your Aunt Catherine has been to visit you, I understand. She immediately returned to Rosings but I persuaded her to allow Anne to remain. She is blooming as I have never seen before.

I congratulate on your forthcoming marriage. I assume it is not a great match by material standards, but then I wager you have more of the Fitzwilliam in you and always believed you would marry for affection.

My wife was invited by Miss Bingley, who we understand is sister to your host in Hertfordshire, to visit and meet the Bennet family. My wife had wanted to throw you a betrothal ball but Richard was especially keen to accept Miss Bingley's invitation. I fear you may be in for some teasing by your cousin but I am certain this is more to your tastes. The whole family will arrive in two days time.

R. Fitzwilliam

Georgiana sat between her new friends and read her letter with wide, disbelieving eyes. How had she been taken in by such false friendship?

My dearest Georgiana,

I was so surprised to hear of you and Mr. Darcy going away with my brother last week, but as I know an announcement which we have all longed to hear will soon follow, it fills my heart with joy to see your continued intimacy with my brother.

You have no equal in beauty, elegance and accomplishments and you know Charles admires you greatly. Beware, though, for Charles is so capable of engaging any woman's heart that I am much mistaken if there is not a young lady in your new neighbourhood who has designs on him. But never fear, dear, Louisa and I will arrive in two days time to spend Christmas at Netherfield and there we will protect our common interests.

I have heard of your brother's engagement to Miss Elizabeth Bennet of Longbourn and I was fortunate enough to meet with your aunt, Lady Fitzwilliam, the other day and invited the entire family to spend the holidays with us at Netherfield.

Yours,

C. Bingley

Bingley happily accepted his letter from his sister and began it with eagerness. He still hoped to have her come to Netherfield. His desires wavered after reading her words.

Charles,

What is the meaning of returning to Netherfield? Why did you not inform Louisa and me? Who is to escort me to the holiday functions? And to know you took Mr. Darcy with you, only for him to propose to that horrid Eliza Bennet, and now he is lost from me forever!

But, I will be kinder to you than you were to me. I am happy that Georgiana went with you, for surely you see Jane Bennet is nothing compared to her. It is of no matter though. Louisa and I will make a very early start and arrive just after breakfast in two days to winter with you at Netherfield. We have the compliment of the Earl and Countess Fitzwilliam arriving on the same day to spend the holidays at Netherfield and meet the Bennet family, and my early arrival will allow me to prepare for our honoured guests; please ensure you are available. I only wish it could all take place in London so Eliza may be properly ostracized, but then on second thought I would not want Mr. Darcy to lose his position in Society, so it is better for Lady

Fitzwilliam to mould Eliza how she must before they arrive in London.

Yours,

C. Bingley

When finished all five looked at each other in amazement and spoke in unison. "Two days time!"

"William, please!" Elizabeth cried.

Darcy was pacing around the library at Longbourn. "No, 'tis too much! Miss Bingley attempting to marry off my sister while she is still a child! Your uncle wanting to *pay* me to marry you! How can it be that strangers, who do not even know me, are inclined to doubt my honour so implicitly!"

Mr. Bennet interjected, "Darcy, really. Gardiner did not doubt your honour, he only wished to not affront your pride, which you have admitted you have."

"But the reputation of your daughter—even your whole family's—was at stake! Even had I not such an attachment to Miss Elizabeth, I could not have walked away!"

Elizabeth came toward him and placed her hand on his arm. "Please, it is all my fault. If only I had not been so prejudiced and unguarded in my writing. Can you ever forgive me for causing so many to believe the worst of you?"

"You at fault! No, no. It was my own actions that encouraged that belief." Darcy sighed. "And it is my pride that is offended again as a result."

Elizabeth smiled slyly. "Perhaps I will save your reputation again!"

Entirely forgetting Mr. Bennet's presence he leaned in for a kiss, before hearing the older gentleman clear his throat.

"I must meet with Mrs. Bennet." Looking at his daughter and Darcy he admonished, "Do not tarry long."

In Mrs. Bennet's chambers, Mr. Bennet found his wife staring off into space.

"Fanny?"

"Oh, Thomas! An earl and countess? Here? The girls! Can they behave?"

"Do you not believe they have learned much in the last fortnight? We have no reason to believe Darcy's family is hateful; they surely cannot expect much from the match as they have never heard of us before. Now, let us use our Bennet pride to some good. We will not be put down by anyone, but we can acknowledge when one is of superior rank. More than that, Kitty and Lydia will not be able to participate in all the adult functions as they are no longer considered out. Besides, Darcy is not changing his mind."

"I must meet with Hill and call on Lady Lucas. Oh, dear. How many are coming? I am certain Bingley will host us at Netherfield some, but the first dinner must be here."

Mr. Bennet smiled at his wife and left her to her tasks.

Thursday, December 19, 1811

Netherfield

11 am

Bingley arose early as his sisters and brother were expected to arrive shortly after breakfast. He had already seen to it all, with the help of Darcy and Georgiana. The rooms were ready for their guests, but he knew Caroline would desire to look things over as well. Although usually, given to sleeping late, he knew Caroline would arrive on time for hosting the Fitzwilliams. They were all invited to dinner at Longbourn.

"Charles! How could you allow this to happen?" Caroline cried as soon as she saw her brother.

"Keep your voice down!"

"I simply do not understand it. Darcy was more than happy to leave the area when we departed and he fervently agreed with me on the matter of the Bennets, and yet only a few days later he returned and I hear in Town he was engaged to Eliza all that time? Why would he conceal the engagement? It is so unlike him to lie, or even omit things!"

Bingley was growing nervous. Who knew what Caroline would concoct to explain this discrepancy or when she might voice it?

"Have you never wanted to veil your true opinion of things? Perhaps affection for someone? We all know you never had romantic feelings for Darcy." Caroline blushed, and Bingley continued, "I hope you had a pleasant drive, but I do believe Mrs. Clark needs your help in the blue room."

"Oh! Why did you not say so earlier? All must be well for the Co...the Countess!"

She scurried off and Bingley released a sigh, before finding Darcy to apprise him of his concerns.

He found his friend in the library.

"Darcy, I need to speak with you."

"Very well."

"Did you and Lizzy discuss how to present your engagement?"

"I proposed the night of the ball and left for London to settle matters."

"That is all very well, but Caroline has determined that it makes no sense for you to conceal your attachment from her."

"I suppose the notion that I simply did not wish to hear her vitriol would not cross her mind?"

"No, and I daresay you cannot respectfully say that to her face."

Darcy sighed, and Bingley understood it all. Darcy hated fake civility and had certainly needed to use it constantly on Caroline. Bingley continued his point. "I worry what reason Caroline has formed in her own mind, and what she may say to others. We cannot rely on her to be guarded in her statements."

"What do you mean?"

"Well, the correspondence is known here and, if there is no reason to think that you were not engaged when they were sent, then it is of no concern. But I fear she will imply the engagement happened due to scandal."

Darcy scoffed. "First of all, she was much more aware than Elizabeth was of my admiration. Secondly, I doubt she is foolish enough to question my honour to my face or in front of my noble relatives. Lastly, my uncle brings Arlington with him. She will be far too distracted with a viscount to worry about me at all."

"You do sound confident. Do you really think you can understand her better than me?"

"Charles, I do not mean to insult you or your sister, but the only way I have tolerated her so well all these years is precisely by understanding her and knowing what to say to have some peace. I could almost feel sorry for my cousin, but he can fight for himself. Besides, Miss Bingley is not so terrible. I daresay she is not very different than me, she is quite aware of her duty to the family to marry well. Perhaps one day she will, like me, learn that affection is superior to consequence."

"Well, then I will have no worries."

"Come, let us prepare for the afternoon. When do you announce your engagement to Jane?"

"She has asked to inform my sisters."

Darcy raised his eyebrows, and the two friends laughed and readied themselves for all the pomp and circumstance Miss Bingley would roll out for the arrival of Darcy's family.

Thursday, December 19, 1811

Longbourn

At five o'clock the entire Netherfield party arrived at Longbourn, nearly bursting it at the seams. Elizabeth sat nervously in the drawing room as Darcy introduced his family.

"May I introduce my uncle, Lord Robert Fitzwilliam and his wife, Lady Eleanor Fitzwilliam? Aunt, Uncle this is Mr.

and Mrs. Thomas Bennet and their daughters Jane, Elizabeth, Mary, Catherine and Lydia."

He paused to allow Mr. Bennet to speak. "We are very pleased to meet you and honoured to have you in our home. Allow me to introduce my wife's brother and his wife, Mr. and Mrs. Edward Gardiner of London."

Elizabeth held her breath, fearing looks of disdain from Darcy's family towards her London relations, but they all looked pleased to make the acquaintance.

Darcy spoke with surprising civility to the Gardiners, despite his earlier affront at the letter, and then spoke again to the whole room. "Allow me to also present my cousins: Joseph, the Viscount Arlington, Richard, a colonel in the royal Horse Guards Blue, Lady Emilia and Lady Alice Fitzwilliam and Anne, the daughter of Lady Catherine de Bourgh."

There was an awkward pause after the greetings but the earl burst forth. "I very much like this room, it is very comfortable!"

Everyone smiled and relaxed, breaking into small groups before dinner was announced. Elizabeth was surprised to see Caroline so easily gave up attending to

Darcy in favour of the Viscount, but then it should not have surprised her if Caroline frequently cared for only the highest rank in the room. She had some kind of odd, teasing relationship with the Colonel frequently glancing in his direction while speaking with the brother. The Colonel, when not slyly insulting Caroline, was one of the most amiable gentlemen Elizabeth had ever met.

Georgiana, remarkably relaxed, was beneficial in easing the conversation between the younger Bennet girls and Anne, Alice and Emilia. Jane and Mrs. Gardiner easily conversed with Lady Fitzwilliam, and even Mrs. Bennet spoke calmly and rationally. Eventually the Viscount and Colonel broke away from the ladies to speak with the other men. Darcy was listening with keen interest to Mr. Gardiner on Lord Elgin's latest acquisitions of ancient Greek marble, and Elizabeth breathed a sigh of relief. Her betrothed seemed ready to befriend her uncle. Elizabeth was left, for the moment, with making conversation with Caroline and Louisa.

"Miss Eliza! I offer you congratulations on your engagement," Caroline began.

"Thank you, Miss Bingley."

"Such a superb match for you! I was rather surprised to hear the news, for Mr. Darcy hates deceit of any kind and yet he never mentioned the real reason he was so eager to part for London."

Elizabeth smiled. "Perhaps, like understanding how to tease him, your intimacy has not yet taught you his reserved nature. You can certainly understand his desire to keep the engagement a secret, especially when he was uncertain how long his business might take."

Louisa interjected then, "He and Charles were off very suddenly. I suppose he hated being away from you at all."

Elizabeth smiled at the true compliment from Mrs. Hurst. "I assure you, it was keenly reciprocated."

Caroline narrowed her eyes, clearly trying to find some kind of flaw in the argument, but Louisa spoke again. "It was very sly of him to have Charles stay with him so he could be off to Netherfield the instant he was available to return."

"Oh, and Charles was able to spend so much time with dear Georgiana!" Caroline nodded to the girl and smiled in triumph.

"Yes, it must have been a relief to Mr. Bingley to experience the sisterly companionship Georgiana could give in your absence. I am very pleased to gain such a pleasant sister, but of course you know that joy as you are such dear friends with the one you are to gain." Elizabeth glanced at Jane.

Caroline's eyes widened in alarm and she looked to Jane.

Jane, having heard the pre-arranged cue, turned her attention to Caroline and Louisa. "Your brother has made me so happy! My joy is all the better as I know I am bringing pleasure to so many as well. For all my family wished for the match and now with two such *dear* friends, who have always showed me every attention, as sisters my life will be complete."

Louisa stammered some kind of agreement. Caroline looked distressed for only a moment, but seemed to take the news with a fortitude Elizabeth did not expect.

"Happy am I that Charles found himself such an agreeable bride and one who is, as you say, such a dear friend. I can scarcely believe how fortunate I am."

Jane leaned in closer. "I can see your concern, dear Caroline, but have no worries.

Wherever I am mistress there will always be space for you. *I* could never treat *you* wrongly."

Caroline gulped, but before she could say anything in response, dinner was announced and they all moved to the dining room. The Countess and Darcy were seated next to Elizabeth.

"I could not help hearing your conversation with Miss Bingley and Mrs. Hurst, and I must tell you how much I admire your subtlety," Lady Fitzwilliam said to Elizabeth.

"Thank you, your ladyship."

"It is plain for everyone to see how much my nephew cares for you."

"I am pleased to hear it."

"You are much more sly than he."

"Do you mean to suggest I am too reserved in my admiration?" She nearly laughed at the idea that she could be like Jane.

"If he is convinced of it then it is quite enough for me; however, I have seen your relatives cast confused looks at you."

Elizabeth allowed her eyes to find her aunt and uncle, who indeed were looking at her in perplexity, and she blushed. "They were surprised by the news of our engagement."

"I like them very much. I would suppose it natural for them to wonder why a man in my nephew's position would desire to marry a tradesman's niece, but it is you they seem confused about. I daresay they find my nephew infinitely sensible to marry a lady with such beauty, intelligence and talents."

Elizabeth took a sip of wine while she collected her thoughts. Lady Fitzwilliam spoke with kindness but a shrewdness she had not expected. "Thank you, your ladyship."

She took a deep breath and decided on honesty. "Mr. Darcy and I had an unconventional courtship. He believed he owed a duty to his family to marry better, and so he concealed his admiration. I believed he disliked me and all my friends and family. I understand he was surprised by his feelings and, I assure you, so was I. We both masked what we believed was imprudent to feel, we acted accordingly, and spoke unguardedly to others about it. Miss Bingley likely has some stories of Mr. Darcy insulting my origins and, sadly, the whole of Meryton knows of my declared dislike.

"I was also free in expressing my feelings in my letters to my aunt and uncle, but was too embarrassed to write to them of my changed understanding of Mr. Darcy's character and the enlightenment of my own admiration. It was only when Mr. Darcy declared himself, and I understood the true depth of his regard, that I was able to openly reveal my attachment. My Aunt and Uncle are simply very protective of me."

"I am pleased to hear it and thank you for speaking so honestly. My nephew has had a false sense of duty about him. His education was not managed very well due to his parents' death at an early age. He has frequently felt he must be irreproachable and has desired to live up to a very idealized version of his parents."

Elizabeth let out a light laugh. "Forgive me, your ladyship. I was previously convinced your nephew and I were very much alike in many ways, but on this we could not be more different. My own parents never provoked that sentiment in me."

Lady Fitzwilliam cocked her head and looked at Mr. Bennet and then his wife for a moment. "I believe I can understand how it might feel to a child, but I see two very affectionate parents. It is a parent's prerogative to be embarrassing. Allow the Earl to have more than two glasses of port with the gentlemen, on top of this wine, and you shall see why Alice and Milly keep casting me worried looks."

Elizabeth glanced at the parties mentioned and had to stifle her laugh. "Forgive me."

"Nonsense, child. We all laugh over it. We must all have some folly in us."

"Yes, your ladyship," Elizabeth said smilingly brightly.

"Please, call me Aunt Eleanor."

Elizabeth eagerly agreed and the rest of the meal passed, surprisingly, without incident. When the ladies withdrew, Darcy's female cousins sidled next to Elizabeth to speak with her.

After some time, Alice blurted out, "When did you know you were in love with Darcy?"

"Alice!" Emilia chided.

"What? As if you do not wish to know?"

"Well..."

"We certainly do!" Lydia said, joining them, and Elizabeth looked up to see the entire room fixed on her.

Blushing profusely, Elizabeth mumbled incoherently at first. Seeing the confused looks the others gave her, she took a deep breath and tried again. "After one of our arguments, while explaining to myself all the deficiencies in his character, I had a sudden moment of clarity, an epiphany. I had attempted to make out Mr. Darcy's character, but realized my own instead."

Alice frowned. "That is not very romantic."

Elizabeth laughed. "I am afraid *I* am not very romantic."

"Well, then when did you fall in love with him?"

Elizabeth laughed again. "If it was a surprise to learn it then, how would I have known when it happened?" She shrugged her shoulders. "I can only say that I believe my heart knew his even before I understood my own."

"Do you know when he fell in love with you?"

Elizabeth laughed. "I do not think I should say, for it would give you a very poor impression of him."

"Tell!" Alice and Lydia cried together and even Caroline seemed intrigued.

"Well, I am convinced that he could only admire me for my impertinence. In my confused feelings and supposed dislike I treated him very badly, being both impertinent and argumentative, but he is so noble and just he turned my faults around. It is reasonable to think that he was simply tired of those that flattered him, for there was no actual good in me at all."

Elizabeth did not notice the men begin to filter in, or the glances of her audience, until she heard Darcy's voice rather near. "Was there no good in your affectionate behaviour to Jane while she was ill at Netherfield?"

She startled for a moment but recovered quickly, "Dearest Jane! Who could have done less for her? But make a virtue of it by all means. My good qualities are under your protection, and you are to exaggerate them as much as possible; and, in return, it belongs to me to find occasions for teasing and quarrelling with you as often as may be; and I shall begin directly by asking you what made you so shy of me during all that time?"

"You certainly gave me no encouragement."

"*You* might have encouraged *me* more. You never looked like you cared for me and you scarcely talked to me."

"A man who had felt less, might."

"How unlucky that you should have a reasonable answer to give, and that I should be so reasonable as to admit it!"

Smiling at Darcy, she heard her aunt ask the room, in general wonder, "Goodness Gracious! Are they always like this?"

Bingley laughed outright, but Caroline answered, with laughter in her voice. "Always! I daresay they border on incivility to the rest of us."

"Could there be finer symptoms? Is not general incivility the very essence of love?" Colonel Fitzwilliam said while glancing at Caroline, who blushed.

Not perceiving his words could mean anything else, Elizabeth laughed. "It is true,

Darling. It was always as though no one else existed when we would speak." Belatedly she realized she used such an endearment in company but a quick glance around the room showed no one seemed shocked.

"And now you know why I could never be sociable with anyone else."

Elizabeth scoffed in disbelief. "You were unsociable your first night in the country!"

"And you were in the room, were you not?"

Half the room rolled in laughter. Bingley cried out, "Darcy! She was the one I wanted you to dance with!"

"No! No, you pointed to some other lady. Elizabeth sat next to her but she looked much older and different than Elizabeth."

"You did not think you were mistaken in your understanding after we dined at Longbourn and you met all the girls? I told you I wanted to introduce you to Jane's sister!"

"I believed *you* were mistaken!"

The whole room joined in the laughter at that pronouncement. Patting his arm,

Elizabeth breathlessly declared, "That, as you can see, none of us have a problem believing."

Darcy coloured a little. "Perhaps I was not so haughty as you presumed, Dearest, but I had my conceit. I thought highly of my own sense and worth; apparently I could not even acknowledge the possibility that I was mistaken, even then, and to my friend."

Caroline muttered something.

"What was that, Miss Bingley? I could not hear you." Alice asked.

"Oh, it was nothing."

"It sounded like you said my cousin had once declared of Miss Elizabeth, 'She a beauty! I would as soon call her mother a wit.' Is that not what it sounded like to you Milly?"

"Alice!"

"What? Should not Darcy have a chance to defend himself to that statement?"

The room was suddenly very quiet, and Caroline was quite red. "I...I...I am certain I have misremembered," she stammered out.

Darcy waved her off. "There is a

perfectly rational explanation, and it will answer your query from several minutes ago, Alice. I was already quite falling in love with Elizabeth—and before she disliked me so much to be as she calls herself 'impertinent'—and so it is as Richard says, I was horribly uncivil."

He raised Elizabeth's hands to his lips. "Will you forgive me for being so arrogant? I felt I must disguise my attraction."

"It is as I said. I realize now that you were masking your real feelings."

He walked over to Mrs. Bennet and took her hand in both of his. "Will you forgive me for insulting you?"

"We all know I have no wit. Lizzy gets that all from her father. Heaven help you, son."

The Earl staggered from the sideboard, sloshing his glass and then raising it in a toast. "To the future Mr. and Mrs. Darcy, Heaven help you both! Damned fine port you have, Bennet!" The room erupted in laughter.

Epilogue

December 9, 1812

Pemberley

Darcy searched for his wife of nearly one year, letters in hand, and found her in the mistress's study.

"Dearest, I just received the mail and there are letters for you." Before handing them into her open hand, he continued with mock scowl while looking at one. "This is written in a masculine hand, but is not from your father. Tell me, is it your custom to engage in illicit correspondence with gentlemen? Or is there something special about this date?"

She broke into a wide smile at his tease, but simply replied, "Tend to your own letters as I tend to mine, William."

She snatched the letters from his hand and settled on the settee as comfortably as her body, growing heavy with child, would allow. He settled in the chair next to her. She flipped through her stack before setting them aside.

Mrs. Jane Bingley wrote tales of little Charles from their new estate, not thirty miles from Pemberley. Lydia wrote from Rosings. After meeting the year before, she and Anne de Bourgh became fast friends and corresponded for months. At long last Mr. Bennet agreed to allow his youngest daughter, who was greatly improved in temperament, to visit the estate. Elizabeth looked forward to reading her sister's thoughts on Lady Catherine de Bourgh.

Lady Catherine had finally reconciled to the marriage of Darcy and Elizabeth some six months ago. Elizabeth laughed to herself as it was just the time when they announced to the family their suspicions that Elizabeth was with child. How amusing that Lady Catherine and Mrs. Bennet would share the same feelings at the news! Mrs. Bennet was still on the silly side but assured of the love of her husband, the respect of her children, and no longer fearful of the future, she was much calmer and nearing sensible.

Elizabeth knew the letters from Mrs. Gardiner and Lady Fitzwilliam were corroborating dates for spending the Christmas holidays together, once again. This year it was to be at Pemberley. She was so pleased the Earl's family got on well with her family from trade, and that Darcy loved them almost as dearly as he loved her.

The letter from Anne held news of an engagement, or so Elizabeth strongly suspected. Perhaps it was not quite a love match, but Lady Catherine was shrewd. Due to the breach with Darcy, Viscount Arlington was invited to Rosings more frequently. The two were well suited to each other and, more importantly, the relationship was Anne's choice and was not forced on her by others.

Elizabeth smiled at the letter from Mrs. Caroline Fitzwilliam. Caroline and Richard got over their bickering shortly after Elizabeth and Darcy exchanged vows. Released of her bitterness and jealousy, and inspired by the love matches around her, she realized she would rather have affection than consequence and yielded to her admiration of the good colonel. Surprisingly, she proved quite an amiable friend, even when Elizabeth teased her for being smitten with a gentleman in a red coat.

While hearing the faint sounds of Georgiana, Mary and Kitty in the music room, Elizabeth watched surreptitiously as her husband made a great show of leafing through his own letters. She saw a small smile appear on his face as he tenderly traced the direction on one envelope before tearing open the seal.

"And who has written you, to inspire such a look?" She asked in pretend jealousy, and leant towards his chair to espy the handwriting.

He grinned and answered, "An impertinent acquaintance I once thought I would have to give up, but keeping it was the best thing I ever did." His eyes returned to the parchment in his hand as heat began to creep up his face. The letter was decidedly more *affectionate* than the one he had received a year prior.

Glancing towards Elizabeth he was pleased to see she had opened his letter, and was just as affected by his own *loving* words.

"William," said the voice that could still set his heart beating too quickly. "How did you ever love me? I never spoke to you without wishing to give pain. I could bring nothing of worth to the marriage. Had you been perfectly reasonable you never would have cared for me."

"I could ask the same of you, Elizabeth. You knew no actual good of me."

"Now, be serious," she said, even as she leaned closer from her seat.

He answered with a teasing smile she could never resist. "I will if you will." He took her nearest hand, drawing circles on it as he leaned even closer to her.

"Perhaps we might answer at the same time?" She smiled at the game they had often played in the last year. She closed the gap between them, touching their foreheads together.

"I knew you by heart," they replied in unison. Their lips met and it was some time before either could speak again as they were much more agreeably engaged.

The End

Acknowledgments

This story was inspired by a short challenge piece for an online forum in Autumn of 2013. Since then it has been through over two dozen edits and rewrites and I must thank the encouraging members of BeyondAusten.com, A Happy Assembly, and DarcyandLizzy.com for their kind words. A special thank you goes to Jim, Linda, Kimberley and Sophie for their wonderful and tireless editing; to Sarah for encouraging me to expand this story and make it even better; and to Rosie for last minute consultations and soothing of frazzled author nerves.

Thank you to the countless other people of the JAFF community who have inspired and encouraged me.

Last but not least I could never have written, let alone published, without the love and support of my beloved husband and babies!

About the Author

Rose Fairbanks fell in love with Mr. Fitzwilliam Darcy twelve years ago. Coincidentally, or perhaps not, she also met her real life Mr. Darcy twelve years ago. They had their series of missteps, just like Elizabeth and Darcy, but are now teaching the admiring multitude what happiness in marriage really looks like and have been blessed with two children, a five year old son and a two year old daughter.

Previously rereading her favorite Austen novels several times a year, Rose discovered Jane Austen Fan Fiction due to pregnancy-induced insomnia. Several months later she began writing. *Letters from the Heart* is her second published work.

Rose has a degree in history and hopes to one day finish her PhD in Modern Europe and will focus on the Regency Era in Great Britain. For now, she gets to satiate her love of research, Pride and Prejudice, reading and writing....and the only thing she has to sacrifice is sleep! She proudly admits to her Darcy obsession, addictions to reading, chocolate and sweet tea, is always in the mood for a good debate and dearly loves to laugh.

You can connect with Rose on Facebook, Twitter, and her blog: rosefairbanks.com

Join her mailing list to keep up to date on new releases and sales! http://eepurl.com/bmJHjn

Also by
Rose Fairbanks

The Gentleman's Impertinent Daughter

Undone Business

No Cause to Repine

A Sense of Obligation

Love Lasts Longest

Sisters Bewitched

Once Upon a December

Mr. Darcy's Kindness

Made in the USA
Monee, IL
17 February 2025

12483782R10144